# WELCOME

Welcome Dear Explorer!

I'm so glad you're here! You are about to embark on the transformational magic of LoveBytes — a light-encoded, multidimensional journey home to yourself. The invitation of this New Earth awakening adventure is to help you expand into your highest potential by taking you on an epic, extended healing visualization.

Part of this book's power — and fun :) is the layering of its dynamic light codes. Light codes are a multidimensional way of communication that transmit energy and higher knowing — kind of like a soul spa and system upgrade rolled into one.

So to add another dimension to your experience and receive the book's transformational energies even more easily and profoundly, I have a gift especially for you and the LoveBytes community:

A LIGHT CODE TRANSMISSION AND
ACTIVATION RECORDING!

It's great to listen to even before you begin reading LoveBytes, as it serves as a primer that opens pathways of multidimensional communication and connection. Like the book, it is a living transmission that keeps expanding with you as your frequencies rise. You can come back to both, the book and the recording, again and again to connect to your next level of expansion.

To access the LoveBytes Light Code Transmission and Activation simply go to:

**www.ClaudiaSasse.com/book**

Enjoy your adventure!
Much love,
Claudia

# *Love*BYTES

## A TRANSFORMATIONAL JOURNEY HOME

*Claudia Sasse*

**BALBOA.**PRESS

A DIVISION OF HAY HOUSE

Print information available on the last page.

Balboa Press books may be ordered through booksellers or by contacting:

Balboa Press
A Division of Hay House
1663 Liberty Drive
Bloomington, IN 47403
www.balboapress.com
844-682-1282

ISBN: 978-1-9822-5223-6 (sc)
ISBN: 978-1-9822-5224-3 (e)

Balboa Press rev. date: 03/05/2021

"It is only with the heart
that one can see rightly;
what is essential
is invisible to the eye."

Antoine de Saint-Exupéry

# 1

----

We never knew where the path would take us, yet still we climbed.

Exhausted, I wipe my forehead. Dirt mixing with sweat creating a smeary trail, like a reminder of the trail we had traveled up to this point. The land is tropical, lush, rich — but foreign for someone like me who grew up in the north.

The cacophony of birds is deafening at times. Mocking, teasing, taunting, celebrating, and sweetly soothing, all at the same time. Flowers that remind me of hibiscus, but as large as my head, rest on fleshy leaves. Strangely, there are no insects — at least none of the bloodsucking, biting kind. The air feels layered: there is a light crispness underneath the sweltering, tropical heat.

*Why am I telling you all this, I wonder?*

*I live in two worlds, you see. On one hand, I am traveling up the mysterious path in a jungle unlike any I have ever heard of or imagined. On the other hand, I am sitting on my sheepskin rug, leaning against my bed, typing words into my laptop.*

*"Write!!!" I had heard just as I was waking up, then seeing an image of myself opening my MacBook (with the blue cover that shows every single fingerprint. "Gotta wipe those off," I told myself.)*

*And then I wondered: Is this "writing" prompt a result of my conversation with my friend Melissa, yesterday, after the channeling during our HeartLight Leadership Circle?*

*I am something of an oracle, you see. Except that sounds ancient, and I am really more of a normal kind of woman, at a middle kind of age — a perfect age, actually. What I channel feels like ancient knowledge, though, and brand-new at the same time. A bit like the two layers in the air on that mountain path.*

*So yesterday, my third-grade aspiring author-self got resurrected, after bouncing around the idea of writing a channeled novel — because most of my channeling comes in these multilayered, multifaceted pictures, anyway. Oracle style :)*

*And today, I woke up to this prompt to "Write!!!"*

*Wondering why am I telling you all this? It is as mysterious as the jungle path, so let's keep going.*

"Where are we *now*?" I ask my travel companion.

He turns to me, beaming. He actually looks freaking illuminated, and not a bead of sweat in sight on his strong, kind face. Like he walked through the layer of crisp, fresh morning air while I was toiling through the slightly oppressive, weirdly sweet — decayingly sweet — jungle heat.

"Come sit with me for a minute," he invites me. And he points to some rocks that appear seemingly out of nowhere, just like the little clearing on the side of the path where they sit. He takes my hand as he positions himself to face me. I am a sweaty-hot mess, yet he is lighting up even more in front of my eyes, literally looking like a light being. WTF! Wow! He looks at me, his eyes sending beams of light into mine.

"Who *are* you?" I hear myself ask him.

He laughs lightly, sounding carefree — almost giddy — and totally at ease.

"You might not believe me if I tell you," he replies.

"Try me!" I end up sounding more challenging than I intended.

"I am *you*," he says softly, holding my gaze with his crystal-clear, two-layered, two-colored land-and-sea eyes. His eyes have this incredible depth that melts my heart — melts *me*.

I feel myself dissolving into his gaze, into him in a way that I perceive nothing but his eyes, his presence — yet it

Claudia Sasse

feels strangely like I am feeling my *own* presence. *Whew.* I am shaking my head, wanting to make sense of what I think I just heard, but I cannot break the spell. Nor do I really want to. *"I am you,"* the words begin echoing — but not in my head; more in the space that looks like a bright bubble, and has appeared around us on our seat on the rocks.

All of a sudden, the atmosphere in the bubble changes, the bright sun dims, and stars begin appearing in a night sky. And not any old night sky, but the most breathtakingly beautiful night sky I have *ever* seen. My mouth gapes open as I get up and slowly turn in a circle, eyes cast upward at the dazzling light-show that reaches all the way down to the ground. It's like I am in a planetarium, except it feels as huge as another Universe.

"Whoa!" Bewildered, speechless, I sit down to face him again, immediately drawn back into the spell of his intensely kind eyes. In my head, a million questions are swirling like scraps of paper in a tornado: *"What is this? How did you do this?"* being just the most obvious. It makes me dizzy. Then suddenly they stop, as if someone turned off the twister, and all those scraps of paper gently and gracefully float to the ground, resting at my feet. A peaceful, spacious stillness is all I can feel, and none of the questions and strange occurrences matter anymore.

*I am you!*

There is a presence that is all-encompassing, as if I had not known before what it meant to be truly present, and instead had existed on a sliding scale between "Sorry, not here at all" to "Mostly present, but still a bit distracted — just in case."

*"In case of what?"* I snap back to my place at the laptop, as if the presence that I am beginning to feel as I tell the story is too much. As if I have to stay in the "real," rational world. I

*listen to the sweet morning song of the birds, my mind going on its familiar wanderings, my attention towards a cup of tea.*

*"Stay with me." I hear a faint echo.*

*I take a deep breath, postpone the tea, and dive back into the story....*

I "arrive" back in the universe under the stars, primly sit down on my rock, smooth down my clothes, and look up.
"Where were we?" I ask.
He looks at me, shaking his head softly, with the sweetest smile on his face. And I feel myself soften, and melt into his incredible presence again.
"Will you trust me?" he asks.
The question is clear. I can sense no weight around it, no hidden agenda, no weirdness.
"Will you trust me?" he repeats.
My mind does a few somersaults, triple axles, and throws in a rollercoaster ride for good measure. Meanwhile, he quietly waits for my answer, emanating a grounded kind of peacefulness. None of this feels wacky at all, as a matter of fact.
"Ok," I inhale. And then I exhale deeply, as if I need to make space for a new kind of air.

*"This book will change my life" briefly floats through my writer's head, and....*

I am back — back in presence. Which is a weird thing to say, as presence just *is*. Like, there is no "back to" or "away from." It simply *is*. A state of beingness: always around us, in us, with us — always us. We only have to tune in.
How did I *know* this, suddenly?

Claudia Sasse

Overwhelming love begins to course through my heart as he places his hand in the middle of my chest, ever so slightly rocking it back and forth once, as if to make sure it is properly anchored. I almost feel like I am going to faint. "Breathe with me," he says quietly. I lock eyes with him and allow myself to relax into the calm and steady rhythm of his breath. The tension of the overwhelm begins to fade, and I feel myself expanding into the lightest, most spacious state I have ever been in, making room for all this love that is flowing through me.

"*This* is you," he says. "I *am* you, *and* I am mirroring you back to you, so you can experience yourself — the incredible, total, and complete love that you are. The beautiful universe you see around us is *your* universe. I am simply making it visible for you."

*And with that, he vanishes . . . shoots through my head. And I am noticing myself going, "No, no, no, you can't go. The story is just beginning. I don't even know your name, yet!"*

"It's J," I hear.

"Wait, wait, 'J' what? Like 'J.', or 'Jay', or 'JC'?" There is definitely a JC-ness about him.

"No need to call me 'JC,' J is fine," he smiles as he fades from my view.

*I sit there, kind of stumped and speechless in both my worlds. Without J's steady presence to help me create more space and grounding, the sensation of overwhelm grows stronger again. Apparently, I am living this book — at least the energy of it. Oh boy! "Breathe!" I remind myself.*

"And sometimes it's totally ok to take a nap in the middle of the day to integrate all of this. Breathe!" I hear.

# THE MAGIC YOU ARE TO ME

You are a deep and magical space for my
soul to land and be at peace.
Heart bursting open, expanding beyond
limits whenever I meet yours.
Weaving, dancing, soaring, exploring
entirely new dimensions with you
In an adventure I've never known to be possible.
Recognizing in you what already exists within myself.
Breathing in the expansion, the magnificence,
Not willing to shrink back into the safety and
familiarity of a smaller version of myself.
Learning to embrace the perfection of the unfolding.
Eternally grateful we have found each other.

# 2

"Where I have been, no one will go."

*"What's that about?" I wonder. By now, I am becoming more used to these seemingly random bits and pieces, with the direction to write them down. My computer's autocorrect feature just turned the word "write" into "co-write" — and, yes, that's what it seems like. I am co-writing this with . . .. whom? Is there an answer? No, not really. Whenever I do my work as an intuitive guide, it's similar: I receive images and messages with the directive to convey them before I necessarily know where it will go, or how it even makes sense. We always find out in the end, and I know it's always from the highest, most loving and expansive energy. I trust that. And no, I don't need a name for it.*

"Where I have been, no one will go, *ever!*" Furiously, she stomps her foot, revving up to an eardrum-shattering scream of total hysteria.

I look at her bewildered, layers of dream journeys softly wafting in. Am I to stop her hysteria? I take a breath and keep looking, just watching her. She is wearing a soft, light pink jacket that looks like a cross between a cuddly bed throw in a girl's room and an Easter bunny. It's quite a stark contrast to the fuming thunderclouds she is spewing. I keep looking at her.

"Hi," I say softly and raise my hand in a hint of a wave. I sound more like her fluffy jacket than matching her undeniable anger and frustration. She whirls around, incredulous but somehow interrupted in her stream of hysteria. She had not known I was there.

Well, neither did I, really. *"Where-am-I-who-are-you?"* I think almost automatically, while being pulled back a little into the energy of a dream I just left and can't quite remember — trying to hold on to its strands, which blow like soft pink ribbons around me. Hmmm, their color matches her jacket....

Am I inside a dream? And what *is* a dream, anyway? She raises her hand to greet me.

"Oh hi," she says, smiling and a little out of breath. She grabs a tall white paper cup from the small folding side table next to her with iron legs and wooden slats, and takes a sip. "I didn't see you there. Are you from the agency?"

As my eyes zoom out a little, I finally notice where I am. I am standing on a stage with her. *"Is this a big theater?"* I wonder. I can't tell, as its size appears to change from huge to intimate all the time. I guess it's not important.

"No, I am not from the agency," I reply. "Actually, I have no idea why I am here. Do *you* know?"

She begins to smile, her smile growing wider by the second — and now she is flat-out beaming, like a little girl who gets to show her *favorite* toy to her best friend, excited about all the play and adventures they will have with it together.

"Hi again, I am Laura," she says, as if she has just landed back in her body with both feet steady on the ground as she walks over to me and enthusiastically shakes my hand. *"Welcome!"* she announces.

"Welcome to where, exactly?" I ask.

"To the *Theater of Your Life!*" she proclaims, waving her hand with a theatrical flourish, in the opening half-circle of a circus director or introductory presenter before they leave the stage to the performer. For a second, I am afraid she will do just that: walk off the stage. But she takes another sip of her drink and sits cross-legged on the floor. "Come sit," she invites me, patting a spot on the floor next to her.

Yet before I can follow her invitation, she changes her position, and she *keeps* changing it until she is spinning in a circle so fast that she looks like a whirlwind. There is that tornado again...! I'm just standing there, shaking my head, when she comes to a stop.

"Sorry," she says, laughing and slightly out of breath once more. "I am just having so much fun doing this. I will hold still now, I promise. Come sit right next to me."

Before I can crouch down on the dusty stage floor, we are transported into the third row of the audience. Good! Those plush red seats are definitely more comfortable. It's a good-size theater, now, and somehow I feel like she and I are a (dream) team, here to produce a show.

The word "director" keeps flashing through my head. Am I the director of this play, or whatever it is? I guess it would make sense if this is the Theater of My Life. Laura somehow reads my thoughts and bounces up and down in her seat. Gosh, this girl is excitable! I have to laugh; and once I start, I can't seem to stop until both Laura and I are a giggly heap.

"See, it's not so serious, it's fun!" she beams, smiling brightly and at the same time revealing an incredible warmth and wisdom, which feels ancient and true, in the depth of her blue eyes.

"Now what, Laura?" I ask, turning towards her.

"Right!" she says catching her breath yet again, this time from all the giggles. "'Now what?!' It's actually up to you. It's your theater. It's your life. I'm just here to assist."

My heart drops. I almost feel nauseous. Shit! I don't know "now what." How am I supposed to know?

"Take a breath!" Laura orders. "Close your eyes and take a breath. I am right here, and I am not leaving you."

Ok. Breathing . . . deeply . . . but I am feeling myself going unconscious, floating off somehow.... My eyes snap open — exaggeratedly wide-open — in the way you might see on people who panic or try to stay awake while driving their car at night.

"It's not helping, Laura," I whine.

She looks at me lovingly. "You can't screw this up, you know," she says softly.

"But if this is the theater of *my* life, I can screw all *kinds* of things up." I am flat-out scared now.

*"What if I'll never make it on my own? What if I will always depend on others? What if I never really get to share my gifts with people? What if I remain trapped in my own life? What if there is no money to ever flow into my life aside from the $19.01 I have left in my bank account?"*

I am actually only thinking all this, but Laura can obviously hear me clear as day. She takes both of my hands into hers and looks intently at me with her soulful blue eyes, which now look like deep wells.

"Do you remember what J transmitted to you about presence?" she asks quietly.

"Wait, what?? How do you know about J?" But I am only surprised for a split second. Of course she would know about J.

"Yes, yes I do," I nod.

"Take a breath and go to that place that is no place, only IS-ness. Allow for all your 'what ifs' to be there if they want, and simply observe. Be with them, like you were watching my meltdown on stage before."

How did she...? Never mind. Ok, I inhale deeply, and this time I feel much more relaxed. As I close my eyes and breathe quietly, I notice how the swirling thoughts begin to quiet down and eventually make space for . . . space. I notice a spaciousness emerging — light, expansive, and clear — seemingly hovering above the swampy, dense place I had been in when I was panicked. Yet this space is not hovering in nothingness; it *is* connected to . . . hmmm . . . to me. It feels grounded, but grounded within myself.

Claudia Sasse

Wow, this is different from anything I ever learned about "grounding." Could a person be grounded in spaciousness and lightness, then?

"Yes," Laura says. She startles me; I still am not used to her telepathic abilities. I smile at her, feeling at peace now, noticing the faintest hint of excitement bubbling up, and still breathing into this present moment. "It will get easier, you know," she says. "Right now, you still need to pay attention. But the more you bring yourself back to the here-and-now with your breath, the more being present will *be* like breathing — effortless and natural — your connection to life itself on this planet."

# PEACE

The sky is grey, the hill in the distance just the shadow of an idea.
No clarity of what is to come. Yet this moment
is peace, paradise, perfection.

The ocean is calm and smooth.
Waves steadily rolling in like liquid steel.
The usually relentless wind is calm this morning
and there is a hint of warmth in the air.
You can feel the strength of the brilliant sunlight behind the clouds.

Birds are resting on the sand, on the water, occasionally flying
up to perform one of their kamikaze dives to catch a fish or sail
across the waves to explore a different corner of paradise.
Even the vultures feeding on a dead seal just a
reminder of the perfection of the circle of life.

Dolphins arching alongside.
Keeping pace in the water with my footsteps on the sand.
Stopping and playing in front of me as I
stop and "play" for a little while.
Picking up their travels as I head on.

There is such peace all around in this grey moment.
My inner and outer space gently moving in and
out of each other in a calm, graceful dance.
The future, the distance, the bright light — it's all veiled.
What matters is HERE. What matters is NOW!

# 3

I stay in my theater seat, not wanting to do anything or go anywhere. This presence thing is sweet. A thought is floating in . . . *wouldn't I need to take some kind of action eventually?* But it does not really matter, it seems. Instead, I see rings emanating from me, like the rings that form when you throw a stone into still water. These particular rings look more like a mixture of light and matter, though. Small grey particles like dust or sand are floating in rings of golden light.

*Many of my morning hikes have taken me to a beautiful valley on the north shore of the Big Island of Hawaii, where I have been guided to move recently. It feels incredibly sweet and loving down there — like Mama Hawaii is letting you sit in her abundant lap while simply embracing and loving you.*

The scene changes, and Laura and I are transported right there, to my favorite spot by the river. I keep seeing those rings emanating from me — stronger now, in higher frequency. I want to pay attention to what is happening with Laura, but I literally can't. I am caught in the intensity of my own emanation — or maybe it's a transmission? Who knows, but it is intense. So, I am simply being present with *that*.

*I love that we are out in nature again in the story, now. Being in nature is always so powerful. How have we humans lost our deep connection with that?*

"You are *always* doing that, you know?" Laura's voice cuts through the intensity.
"Doing what?"

"Sending out signals like that. It is up to you how clear the transmission is, though."

I notice how the color of the rings changes into a crystalline white. I continue seeing myself in the middle of it all, breathing, as they change yet again, now becoming wider fields incorporating beams of white light. I have no thought, no desire. I am simply observing how a field of crystalline white light is being created around me.

*The sensation is beginning to spill over, and I am in such an intensely relaxed state that it is becoming hard to type. Yet I keep going.*

A white-golden sun above gets my attention for a moment, looking like its rays are mingling with my field, ultimately creating a golden border around it like a frame. Breathing, I notice a sense of sweetness and freedom beginning to fill me and then spill out into the space.

I am feeling more at home with the intense energy within those rings of light now, and getting curious about the sun. It is not like the "normal" sun that I am used to: I can actually look at it. I also notice that the valley doesn't quite feel and look the same as usual. I have the odd sensation of being in something like a hologram.

"You are in the Space Between," Laura explains, "where possibilities become realities."

"Interestingly enough, I don't even flinch at this strange piece of information. "Oh, ok," I answer. "Tell me more." At the same time, I can feel how my heart is stirring, like it's expanding as sweet soft love washes through me. The feeling reminds me of Laura's fluffy pink jacket, and makes me smile.

"What do *you* know?" Laura asks. "About the Space Between? What do you know?"

"How am I supposed to...?" I begin to protest, but then close my mouth again. What if I *do* know something? I close my eyes, take a breath and focus. It's more like I relax into focusing. Interesting....

A scene begins forming in front of my inner eyes. I see breathtaking stars in the night sky. I see giant reddish-brown sand dunes with beautiful lines, chiseled and soft at the same time. I see an old pocket watch. I see a desert vehicle in the distance with people on it, like out of a "Mad Max" movie....

Now my head whips to the right and I have the sensation of being accelerated like a spaceship through . . . what? Hmmm . . . a time warp, a worm hole? And now I see a black octagonal spaceship landing softly on golden sand. The scene feels peaceful and illuminated. The spaceship is contained within itself, yet still part of the whole scene, which also feels peacefully contained within itself. I am curious what might unfold, yet wondering, "What on Earth this all has to do with the Space Between?"

I am standing next to the spaceship, now. A flap opens and, almost like a one-person greeting committee, a man who looks very much like Morpheus from the Matrix emerges — sunglasses, long leather coat, and all.

"Do you like my fierce starship-commander travel look?" he asks with a mock scowl. And then he throws off his coat and glasses, which instantly disappear, to reveal a soft sand-colored long-sleeved shirt and loose pants out of the same material, which seems to be a mixture of linen, silk, and cotton. It looks comfortable, and kind of sexy on his muscular body.

"Come sit with me," he invites me with a big bright smile, very much at ease. We find ourselves in a wide valley surrounded by a low yellow-golden mountain range. The expanse of sand that we are standing on lights up in the most glorious evening sunshine. I must be getting used to those quick changes of scenery; I don't skip a beat but simply follow the invitation.

"My name is C," he introduces himself in a deep resonant voice that *totally* sounds like Lawrence Fishburne.

"C for 'Commander'?" I ask, and he smiles.

*I am sitting on my sheepskin rug, scratching my head. Where the heck is this story going? "Don't fight it, just write it," I hear. Cute! But I doubt myself. Am I doing this right? Am I spinning off on some weird tangent? Is this getting out of control? It certainly is not following any of my expectations.*

*Aaah yes, there they are — those lovely words: "control" and "expectations." I know they have never been helpful. When I think back about my efforts to control any situation or have any of my expectations met, they pretty much have always resulted in a face-plant of some sort. And really, "control" and "expectation" are the opposite of presence, aren't they? "Keep on going. You are doing just fine," I hear.*

*Yes, but first — breakfast :)*

When I return, C pulls a stick out of the air (of course) and draws three concentric circles into the glowing sand.

"Look at those," he says, pointing. The simple sand drawing looks illuminated and feels Zen, but it's not like it's a never-before-seen major revelation that warrants a spacecraft and wormhole travel. "Go beyond the obvious," he instructs.

"Hmmm, what else is there?" I wonder. Curious now, I keep looking at the circles, and begin seeing symbols between the grains of sand. Looking something like geometric hieroglyphs, they crowd the space between the indentation made by the stick when C drew the circle, while all I can perceive *in* the actual circle is regular sand. The symbols are in constant motion, and almost look like they are "talking" to each other.

"Yes," C says. "They are actually communicating."

"So, who is 'they'? What are those symbols?" I am definitely intrigued.

"Those are light codes," C explains.

I keep wanting to call him Morpheus. And I can sense how he's searching for a way to transmit something in the

Claudia Sasse

most effective way that otherwise might be complicated for a human brain to grasp.

"Light codes can be sensed more than read. They are a multidimensional way of communication, and they transmit feelings and higher knowing."

As I keep looking at the light codes dancing before my eyes, I can feel that sweet soft love washing through me again.

"What you are feeling is what I am transmitting to you right now, as much as you are feeling the same being activated within yourself."

I sit with this information for a moment, just being still and allowing the sensation to take over. I can feel my heart expanding, again. The extent of the expansion feels unfamiliar, almost uncomfortable, like I am entering new territory. I simply stay with it, though, breathing. I sit there smiling, floating in the sweetness and softness for a while, and eventually I turn back to C. "Can you tell me more?"

"Feel this," he says, as the image he drew into the sand begins lifting up and turning into a three-dimensional structure in constant motion within itself, and completely surrounding me. In actuality, it feels like it has more than three dimensions, and like the structure is flowing not only around me but also through me, although I can't perceive that with my eyes. What I notice, though, is that my heart sees, my heart understands — all of it!

I can see-feel how my world is getting bigger. New universes are opening up, flowing through each other, much like the ring structure. Day and night are in constant flow, sometimes happening simultaneously. Scenes pop in and out of my view, constantly changing. It feels vast, expansive, beyond comprehension, yet my heart is at home here. I feel happy, almost giddy.

I try to think of something I'm worried about and literally can't. Wait a second. How weird is that? As I am floating in total bliss, I am trying to think of something to worry about. Really? It seems so ridiculous that I literally laugh out loud.

"I know, it seems funny, doesn't it?" C smiles. "Humans do it *all* the time, though — contracting into familiar worry and fear. It's part of the survival mechanism that was quite necessary on Earth for a while. So now it is a cellular memory as much as a 'safety' habit.

"Let me show you what happens. Just as there are light codes, there are also dark codes." The beautiful light-play of the rings stops, and a darkness that feels as thick as tar envelops us without any warning. Instead of the beautiful expansion, I feel a contraction that weighs incredibly heavily on my heart. It constricts my whole body, actually, and pulls tighter and tighter.

But despite the all-consuming darkness, I can see the rings back on the ground, now displaying black codes on black sand that look distorted, somehow. But I have a feeling that I am not really seeing through the darkness with my physical eyes. I feel like I just want to curl up in a ball and be done with all of this. I don't even have the strength to protest.

After what feels like an eternity, the scene reverts all the way back to the original glow of the setting sun.

"OMG, C, that sucked! Was that really necessary?" *Now* I have the strength to protest again.

"This was actually only a 'normal' dose of worry that most people experience every day," C says evenly. For thousands of years, humans have been operating with a fairly dense carbon-based DNA that is very much in resonance with the dark codes that were aligned with the survival requirements on Earth. This dynamic has been changing, whereby new crystalline DNA strands that are in resonance with the light codes are being activated in more and more people. It has been amplified since 2012. We are talking about an energetic occurrence that is not quite visible under a regular microscope.

"Those of you whose crystalline DNA has been activating, and who have been attuning to the light codes, have a very difficult time with the dark codes now, as you have continuously

Claudia Sasse

been expanding into lighter and lighter realms. So something that might have felt totally normal say, 20 years ago, now completely knocks your socks off with its heaviness. It's like doubling the gravity on your planet, so you can hardly move. "Many kids are being born with their crystalline DNA and their light codes already highly activated. Adults who are becoming attuned to the light codes might often talk about their awakening, their ascension path, or being a light worker, for example. And even if they don't identify with any of that, they *know* that something is very different. Their intuitive capacities are increasing. They are becoming more and more empathic, which poses an additional challenge whenever they tune into the dark codes that are still around them everywhere, from people individually and the collective energies."

*Right! I am really curious about what C has to say about that one. It can be quite a downer, feeling other people's or the collective energy — often without even being aware that what you are feeling is not your own anxiety or anger, and so on.*

"So how do we navigate this?" I inquire.

"Soften and breathe," he says quietly, as if turned inward. "You can't fight the dark codes, often you cannot even redirect your focus. But you *can* be loving towards your experience, regardless whether you are feeling your own *or* someone else's. Be with it with compassion and love, in that sweet loving energy that I reminded you of after we first sat down. Know that what you are feeling is perfect for that moment, and that by meeting the feeling or experience with compassion and love, you help in dissolving those particular dark codes for all of humanity — because you truly *are* all connected."

Wow, that is not the answer I expected! Yet it feels so sweet, spacious, loving, and . . . free.

Freedom! That really takes me by surprise. It feels like I am being released from the eternal fight of light against darkness and can simply and lovingly BE with whatever is present in my world. It's like a huge weight is being lifted off my shoulders. And somehow I keep thinking of Laura and her sweet, soft pink jacket.

* YOU * ARE * LIGHT *

# 4

And there she is! Sweet Laura appears right there, against the rays of the setting sun — giggly, bouncy, and happy as always. I am thrilled to see her and jump up to give her a big hug. I know we have only just met, but it feels like I have known her forever.

"Actually, you have," she grins.

As always, she answers my unexpressed thoughts and feelings.

I have to laugh. These kinds of conversations are really funny and really cool at the same time, somehow.

"I have?" I ask her. I can't imagine that I would have forgotten such a thing as knowing her forever.

"I am one of your soul sisters. We have spent many lifetimes playing together." Laura seems quite excited to share this information.

Oooh! That feels *so* true. My mind, however, is a bit confused and tries to make sense of what I have just heard. But I let it be and simply focus on what I am feeling in my heart. Here, I am aware of the vastness and the depth of our connection, and I can see our lives weaving through each other, much like the ring structure wove through me earlier. Whatever relationship we share feels big and vast, and makes me really happy.

"This is amazing, Laura," I tell her. "When I look at this relationship through my heart, it feels like not only do we know each other, but at times we *flow into* each other, basically sharing the same space. And in that space, it feels and looks like our hearts are communicating with each other in the most beautiful way. There is so much love there. It's like we are one, while still maintaining our own energy field."

"You are catching on quickly," Laura beams. "It is when our energy fields flow through each other's that I hear your thoughts and feelings — only to the point you are open to it, though," she adds.

Basking in that beautiful space in which we are connected, I cannot even fathom wanting to close off any part of me. What would be the point of that?

"Again," Laura continues, hearing my thoughts, "it has something to do with the survival mechanism, and with the idea of scarcity and lack that is still very present for humans."

"Well, for some it is more than an idea — it is the reality they live in!" I protest. "Wars, famines, natural catastrophes, ... and that is only on a *macro* level where many people simultaneously have the same horrible experience. Then is poverty, sex trafficking, domestic violence, bullying, divorces, accidents.... The list goes on."

"Yes," Laura says very softly, "there *is* all that. And now, can you imagine how any single one of these things would be made better if you closed your heart? Imagine yourself pulling back, closing off, rationing your love, putting up borders instead of staying open and meeting all of this suffering with love and compassion. And yes, I can see how you are afraid of being overwhelmed by being open to all this suffering. But it's important to know that it is not your responsibility to fix it all."

I wasn't expecting that.

"Although," she continues, "you might have a brilliant idea and be inspired to take action — for example, by starting a new venture that provides a solution for one of the many challenges that are present on earth right now. If so, then *follow* that inspiration, that spark. You'll know you are on the right track if it lights you up.

"Or maybe," Laura goes on, "you'll feel the nudge to pick up the phone and call a friend, and then find out that your friend really needed support at that very moment. Fabulous! Or maybe you are simply dissolving the dark codes by being in that energy of loving compassion. Can you see how you need to be open and receptive for *all* these scenarios?"

I notice myself reacting to this information on two different levels. My brain is thinking, *"Being open and receptive to all the suffering in the world must be completely overwhelming. Won't I be crushed by it?"* And yet my heart *knows*.

Knows what? I wonder. Ooooh, and then I get it: by my being in the energy of love and compassion, nothing sticks to me. Everything simply flows through me, and all I can feel is love and compassion.

*Something interesting just happened. I got bitten by a few mosquitoes, and the itching is distracting me to the point where I can't stay with the narrative and the feeling anymore. So my own "suffering" (in quotes because I know it's not "real" suffering) is distracting me from any kind of loving and compassionate feeling, because it seems to require my entire focus.*

"So, Laura, what do I do when I am not feeling good myself?" I ask my new/old soul-sister friend.

*Those 'squito bites are clearly sticking to me, not wanting to flow anywhere — not even with the help of my trusted Hawaiian "Bee Boys After Bite" salve.*

"You allow that," comes her answer in a sweet voice. "Be loving and compassionate with yourself. Ask yourself, 'What do I need right now?' Don't fight it. Instead, allow and embrace the perfection of it. Right now, it's actually getting us to talk about this important point."

*Something I heard author and speaker Kyle Cease say in a video a few days ago pops into my mind. It has to do with enthusiastically embracing the perfection of where we are,* even if it feels anything but perfect. So instead of trying to resist it, what if my reaction to the itching on my arm and hand was: "I SHOULD be distracted by itchy bites right now. I LOVE that these bites are distracting me." It immediately makes me breathe easier.

And now, I even have to laugh: The title I was given for this book, Love Bytes, obviously also sounds like Love Bites. There is definitely humor in that :). Laura giggles and laughs a lot, too. Humor and laughter are such a solvent. So I decide not to take any of this too seriously right now, and to have a quick nap, take a shower, prep some dinner and....

# SOVEREIGNTY PRAYER

Beloved, your power is yours, my power is mine
In its entirety.
I release you in love from all entanglements
So that both of us can grow and expand in wholeness
As the full light that we are.
In gratitude for you, in gratitude for me
So it is!

# 5

"I'm back!" Laura gives me a welcome-home hug.

I relax back into my other world. "You know," I tell her, "sometimes it feels like a lot, being with all this energy, Laura — you inviting me to experience all these new things, and the light code activations, on top of generally feeling everybody's energies more and more. But I don't want to turn away from any of it. I *want* to learn, and I want to lean in. So what do I do?"

"Come, let me show you something," Laura says. "It's girl time, C," she waves at her friend. Then she takes me by the hand, pulling me behind her. We walk a few steps towards a tall curiously round sand dune rising from the flat, wide valley floor. How come I hadn't noticed it before?

As we make our way to its backside, I see a small quiet stream with a bridge made of dark wood leading to a patch of what looks like barren poplars. They stand watchful and tall against a deep blue night sky that's still light enough so only a couple of stars are visible. The scene feels serene and peaceful — soothing. It doesn't even occur to me to inquire how we went from day to basically night within a few steps. I feel drawn to walk across the bridge, and I point to it.

"Is that where we are going?" I ask.

"Yes," Laura nods.

Somehow, I already know that we will find a lake on the other side of the trees.

And there it is! The lake is almost perfectly round, and it mirrors the color of the night sky so that its water looks like silky smooth blue ink. A small well bubbles up in the center of the lake, causing its deep, rich waters to send constant ripples towards the edge. The temperature is perfect, like the air is folding its arms around me in a balmy, sweet embrace.

A big, black, porous rock with an indentation on top that looks like a natural bench invites me to sit on it. As I gaze at the lake from the rock-bench, I begin to feel like its ripples are extending their constant motion through my body, through all of me. It is soothing, balancing, harmonizing. I find myself involuntarily inhaling and exhaling deeply, beginning to feel totally relaxed and at ease. I feel like I am becoming one with the water, with the air, with the rock, while the trees behind me stand like regal guardians, yet softly sway in the breeze at the same time.

Laura quietly sits next to me on a rock that looks like light-grey granite. I turn to her and tell her, "Thank you! I am *so* grateful you brought me here. This feels beyond amazing!"

I don't feel any of the overload I felt earlier, anymore. Quite the contrary: Those ripples are running through me like a calming balm for any frayed nerve endings. At the same time, there is nothing to *be* calmed anymore, because I am simply part of it all — or is it part of me? It doesn't matter. I feel so peaceful. I feel whole.

"This is called the Well of Oneness," Laura says, preempting the question forming in my head. "It serves as a visceral reminder of how we really *are* one with everything, *and* whole within ourselves at the same time. Here, we can *feel* it. It's incredible, isn't it?" She beams, but in a way that's softer and more richly deep than usual.

For what seems to be a very long time, yet no time at all, Laura and I sit on our rocks by the Well of Oneness. Breathing, feeling ourselves flowing with oneness, being whole, just being.

After a while something seems odd to me, though — especially since we are at the Well of Oneness.

"Why did you exclude C by telling him this was a girl's trip?" I ask my companion.

"I wanted you to meet someone and I knew that this meeting would be more related to the world of female experiences."

Being here — with you
Our hearts becoming still
Surrendering
To the impossible peace around us
Why question what is?
What is here NOW
Parting the sea
And diving deeper and deeper
Into this moment
Into the stillness of peace.

# 6

"*Ready to receive? ... Ready to receive...? Ready to receive...?*" The words begin echoing all around me in such a way that I feel immersed in them, almost the same way I was feeling immersed in the Well of Oneness. And then, as if I have been primed long enough, the question begins sounding more like an order: "*Receive!!*"

This almost knocks me out, as if it goes beyond my present capacity to receive that much — whatever "that much" even is. I only remember that recently, when talking to a friend, I announced that I wanted "it all." "*So here it goes,*" I'm thinking. . . .

She rises like Venus out of the middle of the Well of Oneness, and the moon is rising with her, her long gown glistening as if spun out of moonlight. Her fine, beautiful, pale features are even and perfectly proportioned. Her eyes, though ... her eyes.... At first they look empty, black, and hollow to me; but then I see Earth — a tiny version of our beautiful blue planet — slowly spinning in both her eyes, while a third Earth globe rotates before her third eye. I have no idea why I know that this is the Moon Maiden, *or* who the Moon Maiden even is.

"Greetings, Beloveds," she addresses Laura and me, with a voice like liquid moonlight. The sound comes both from the figure in front of us *and* from all around us. "I know my appearance can feel intense for humans. So breathe and allow yourself to merge with the Well of Oneness again."

Easier said than done. Her presence is simply overwhelming.

"Receive....!" The word echoes again — omnipresent, inescapable. Why does this almost knock me unconscious? Receiving should be easy, right? I fix my gaze on the spinning globe in her left eye. It makes me dizzy. *All* of this is making me dizzy.

I realize I need to be breathing! Telling myself to expand and flow with the Well of Oneness instead of trying to figure this out.

The Moon Maiden speaks — or, more accurately, she transmits. A flood of images, information, light codes, frequencies, vibrations, feelings are entering my system. It is non-sortable — a deluge, like all the letters of *The Book of Everything* being lifted off the pages and poured into my form in the most random way. Curiously, though, the dizziness subsides and I begin to feel much more clear and grounded. There is a strange physicality and substance to this transmission, as if I have just been given the building blocks to create anything I desire in my life.

"You have chosen to take on the role of a female on planet Earth in this incarnation," the Moon Maiden lets me know, "and with that, the Creatrix of Life. It is the female form that receives, incubates, and births life. It is the female form that knows the strength of its softness. It is the female form whose waters flow with the tides of the moon. It is the female form that...."

But her echoing voice trails off like the receding tide, and she vanishes back into the Well of Oneness the same way she appeared, taking the full moon with her.

Staring at the spot in awe, wonder, and with a soft kind of focus (as if that could make the Moon Maiden reappear), I am grateful when I feel Laura's hand on my shoulder. It feels like something familiar to hold onto in this wild experience.

".........." I want to say something, but I am literally speechless.

"I know." Laura kneels down, hugging me from behind. And we stay like this for a long while, tears streaming down my face as I take it all in. Saying yes to ALL of it. Saying YES! to life itself.

Claudia Sasse

Eventually I begin feeling a chill in the air that makes me shiver, and I know that it is time to go. But when I get up from my seat on the rock, my shivering increases to the point where my teeth are chattering, almost as if my body is in shock from what it has just experienced. Laura takes off her soft pink jacket and hangs it over my shoulders. I immediately feel cradled in the safety of the sweetest, most loving energy, enveloping me like an embrace. My body begins to relax again, and I am filled with enormous gratitude for my friend.

"Thank you, Laura," is all I can say.

"I know," she replies softly. Both of us put our hands in front of our heart in a prayer position, and bow in gratitude and reverence to the Well of Oneness and the Moon Maiden before we turn around and head back the way we came.

I am sovereign
I am clear
I am powerful
My life flows in alignment
With my highest good
And the highest good for ALL

# 7

C must have sensed our return. "We are over here!" he calls when we get back to "camp."

The voice is coming from behind the spaceship. Curiously, the light has not changed at all, and we find ourselves in the warm luminous glow of the evening sun again. When Laura and I round the spacecraft, we see a group of men relaxing and amicably chatting in a circle around what looks like the setup for a campfire.

"Just in time! Come close," C motions.

All of a sudden, I feel really tired, but C, catching on to my slightly drowsy state, says, "You'll want to be present for this."

Still feeling the lingering after-effects of the intense receiving at the Well of Oneness, I pull Laura's jacket tighter around me. Spotting a smooth, dark, glassy-looking rock behind the circle, up on a slight hill, I sink onto the ground and lean against it. "*Obsidian?*" I wonder. I somehow know that this is a circle that Laura and I are allowed — even invited — to witness, but not to take part in. It feels good — grounding, somehow — to be in the presence of all these men, after the intense experience with the Moon Maiden at the Well of Oneness, and I can feel how my body is beginning to relax. Laura makes herself comfy next to me. She has found a woven blanket somewhere, and offers to share it with me.

*I have a hard time seeing how this scene is going to unfold. Maybe because I am a woman?* "Listen deep within your heart," *I hear; and I soften into gratitude for receiving this story, and for all the beautiful, sincere, loving, courageous, kind, generous, and loyal men out there. Thank you!*

"Thank you all for joining this sacred ceremony." A man I hadn't noticed before, addressing the group, echoes my sentiment of gratitude. He feels to me like he should be wearing a wizard robe, but he looks more like a casual, jeans-wearing Jude Law. I guess Jude Law *did* play the young Dumbledore....

"What will we do?" I hear one of the other men asking.

"We are still waiting for the guardians to join us," the young "wizard" replies. While we all wait, I pay closer attention to the men in the group in front of me. I count twenty-four of them, and they all could not be more different. At least they all look human, but otherwise they run the gamut from a skinny nerdy guy with thinning sandy hair and glasses, to a muscle-packed giant with a long black mane and wild beard. Flamboyant and plain, young and old, fit and potbellied, white, yellow, red, brown, black — it's all there.

My observations are interrupted when a line of men – the expected guardians, I think — appears in the distance and snakes toward the circle. The men are dressed in yellow-and-red straw-like skirts and large circular collars that reach down their chest and back. Their long black hair is oiled and woven into a headdress. They have strips of white fur around their calves and muscular biceps. In their hands, they each hold an unusual white staff that seems to be alive. I can see symbols that remind me of the light codes as they come closer.

The guardians look indigenous, in a non-specific way. They move along gracefully and rhythmically, almost in a dance, chanting and intentionally stomping their feet while keeping their wavy pattern the entire time.

When they arrive at the circle, they move around and form an outer ring, each one lining up with one of the men as if to guard them. The wizard speaks, and now he *is* actually wearing a robe. It is purple and looks ceremonial.

"Thank you all again for having the courage to come here today to transform the power of your trauma into the power of love." He swiftly extends one arm towards the center of the circle and the campfire ignites, burning with a violet flame. Then he swings both arms as if to outline the circumference of the circle, and creates something like an energetic shield around the men and their guardians. The shield has a shimmery translucency and looks very alive.

"This is a very sacred ceremony," the wizard says. "And I commend you for having done your preparations in recognizing and admitting to the trauma that has occurred in your life. May I ask you to take out the paper or object on which you have recorded this awareness? In a moment, I will ask you to surrender it to the sacred Fire of Transformation. Know that you will most likely enter a moment where you will re-experience a version or part of your trauma. If you simply allow the emotions, memories, and sensations to pass through without diving back into the story itself, this will be very temporary. Stay present with whatever you experience, and breathe deeply. The guardians are here to give you a light-code infusion, to reactivate and remind you of the light realms, should you get drawn back into the dark codes of your old wounds. Know that there is immense appreciation and gratitude for your willingness to enter this process of release and transformation, as this will rewrite much of the collective trauma programming and allow many of your brothers to transform the power of their trauma into the power of love, as well.

"May I ask you to step forward, one by one, to enter your personal space of transformation and release your trauma into the fire, while the rest of you stand in active support by remembering the light codes for each other during each of your individual releases. Let us begin the ceremony by offering a prayer of forgiveness to our perpetrators and to ourselves.

"Beloved(s), I forgive you for all the trauma you have caused in my life as I forgive myself for any trauma that I have willingly or unwillingly inflicted upon others.

I release all of us in love from the perpetual entanglement and repetition of the stories of pain, destruction, and abuse of power. The cycle of trauma ends HERE! The cycle of trauma ends NOW!

May the power of the trauma be transformed into the power of love. And so it is!"

The guardians bang their staves on the ground, emphasizing the words "HERE" and "NOW." The wizard nods towards a wiry, dark-haired man holding a folded piece of beige paper standing directly to his right. The man takes a deep breath, steps forward and, standing very straight, submits the paper to the purple flames.

As the paper catches fire, a scene flashes above the fire as if on a translucent screen. I see a big, very angry man with a red face, looking overwhelming and menacing, staggering toward a boy who is maybe eight years old. You can tell the man is drunk. The boy tries to duck and protect himself as the first blow sends him across the room. His cries make the man even angrier, and he continues his brutal beating. Bleeding and broken, the boy is eventually left in a corner on the floor of the wood cabin — the site of the crime.

As the scene plays out, the man by the fire lets out a muffled cry, and his arm shoots up as if to protect his head. I can see his face contort in agony. It is obvious how he is struggling to stay calm, but he manages to eventually fall into a rhythm of deep calming breaths. The other men and the guardians look on intently, the men nodding slightly as if in witnessing acknowledgment.

After a little while, light codes begin flooding the entire space, erasing the scene on the screen, replacing it with pure light and completely enveloping the man. He visibly relaxes and now looks illuminated, somehow. A warm smile appears on his face as the light keeps intensifying. After a few more moments, the light begins to radiate from him, rippling beyond the shield. When it reaches the spot where Laura and I are sitting, I can actually feel it. Pure, clear, sweet love envelops me, embraces me. It feels comforting, supportive, free, spacious, grounding, all-accepting, powerful, and clean. Love without expectations or agenda.

One by one, the men step forward; and scenes of every imaginable hurt, abuse, betrayal, and injustice flash in front of our eyes as each one surrenders the record of his awareness into the fire. We see boys stuck in the terror of their parents' divorce, ripped from parents, beatings, sexual abuse, torture, bullying, hazings, and broken hearts. I get the sense that we are only seeing the tip of the iceberg, and that all this suffering goes back for generations and generations. Some men collapse under the intensity of their experience and activate the dark codes of their stories again, but the guardians swiftly step in and jolt them back into the realm of the light codes. They do this by offering one end of their staff, which creates a flash of light that almost shocks the man back into the light realms as he grabs it, like those defibrillation paddles used to reactivate the heart. Yet, one by one, their trauma is transformed into the most beautiful and powerful love energy.

I am filled with gratitude, and am in pure awe of the strength and courage of these men, and their willingness to break the perpetual cycle of suffering and hurt and turn it into love. The ripples of light and love they are generating keep washing over me, and I simply open my heart as wide as I can to receive it.

Visibly moved, the wizard addresses the group again once the last person has finished his transformation. "What you have done today is unprecedented," he says, his voice rich with emotions. "*This* will ring in a new era of freedom, compassion, and love for your planet. My gratitude is beyond words, but I trust you can feel it."

"*YES!! THANK YOU!!*" I think, as tears of gratitude run down my face.

Beloved(s), I forgive you for all the trauma you have
caused in my life as I forgive myself for any trauma that
I have willingly or unwillingly inflicted upon others.
I release all of us in love from the perpetual entanglement and
repetition of the stories of pain, destruction and abuse of power.
The cycle of trauma ends HERE! The cycle of trauma ends NOW!
May the power of the trauma be transformed
into the power of love.
And so it is!

# 8

Slowly, very slowly, I awake from a lingering dream. It blurs my current reality, as if I simultaneously exist in two different worlds. I feel dizzy, unable to bring both my feet down to Earth and ground in either one of them. I allow it, breathing.

*"Writing this book is like that," I think. I am feeling, LIVING the story — and at the same time I am sitting on my sheepskin rug, aware of my normal human form answering a text request on my phone about the MacBook Air I have for sale. It's like weaving in and out of two different worlds. And sometimes that makes me feel a little dizzy. And now we've added another layer — a dreamworld within a dreamworld. Oh boy.*

I actually have no idea where I am, and who is with me, if anyone. The last thing I remember is watching the profound transformations within that circle of men. The lingering dream is about a powerful mountain that feels female and is communicating with me....

*The mountain in the dream feels like Mauna Kea on the Big Island of Hawaii — the tallest mountain in the world. Over 17,000 feet below the surface of the ocean, and over 13,000 feet above. It's where heaven and earth meet: born of fire, while rooted in the ocean waters. It feels so immensely powerful that I cried the first time I ever reached its top, and my travel companion said "THAT is nature." And it made me cry again once I reached the spiritual summit. You feel closer to heaven there — spiritually and physically. The mountain is sanctuary to the Hawaiian people, and gateway into space through the world's most powerful telescopes.*

As I breathe and relax and allow the dizziness to simply be there, I am pulled back — actually, it feels more like I *spiral* back — into the dream. I am walking towards the mountain on a layer of clouds. They not only hold me, they actually propel me forward, almost catapulting me towards a path a little bit below the summit. The path winds through barren rocks that glow in the warm shimmer of a golden red. As I begin ascending, I notice a tall cairn on my left, built with the uneven reddish rocks from around the path. It seems to shift in size and proportion as I get closer — and depending on how I see it.

Huh, depending on how I see it…? That's a knowing that just popped in, but I am not quite sure what that really means. Just before that insight, I thought I got a glimpse of a little being standing (hiding?) behind the rock tower. And for a second, my perspective must have changed into seeing the cairn from its angle, where it would appear like a very tall tower. So for just the tiniest moment, I stepped into someone else's world. "*Walk a mile in someone else's shoes….*" floats through my head.

"Welcome, Dear One." I hear a powerful yet warm and motherly voice. It seems to come from the summit as well as out of the pores of the mountain — like a full-body transmission. "Welcome, Dear One, I am happy that you have chosen to be on this path."

Looking up the path I apparently have chosen, it seems to have gotten steeper, and the summit further away. It actually points straight up, now, which puzzles me. How am I supposed to continue on this path? Yet it keeps shifting, until it eventually begins overextending, the tip of the mountain reaching over my head and starting to create a spiral. Interestingly enough, I am not really concerned, and feel safe in my particular spot on the mountain, while its tip is spiraling down — actually, *reaching* down — to where I stand, meeting me and then sweeping me up.

Claudia Sasse

"Let me make it easier for you, Dear One," I hear.

"Wow," I think-say, "thank you! For a second there, I thought it'd be impossible to reach the summit."

"Take a breath, quiet your mind, let go of your concerns, open your heart, and be with me — just for a minute," I hear the warm embrace of the mountain's voice.

Talking about embrace, I notice that I am still wearing Laura's sweet pink jacket. And then — as if noticing the jacket was my last thought — I am pure presence with the mountain. All thoughts and worries gone — just huge, heart-opening presence. I feel like I am being absorbed by the mountain's magnitude — *becoming* the mountain. It surprises me when I see the tiny little being again that was hiding behind the cairn. It has the warm orange-red-golden color of the rocks, and walks up to me with a big smile.

"Follow your heart and keep following it so fully until that is all you know." The words find me. I hear them, feel them, know them. "Follow your heart so fully until that is all you know…." The words emanate from the rocks around me, enveloping me, spiraling around me, caressing me like a softly whirling wind. "Follow your heart…!" The Rock Being comes closer and begins growing in size as it approaches my spot on the mountain, until it is about as tall as my 5-foot 5-inch frame.

*For some reason, my attention keeps being drawn to the colorful Merkabah Card that I had pulled out of LON's Sacred Geometry Activations Oracle deck the other day, which is sitting on my windowsill. On my lap is the very light, porous, brown lava rock I picked up from a vortex field on Mauna Kea a few days before –- and as I stand up to get the Merkabah Card, the lava rock falls down, slightly disintegrates, and creates a tiny lava-dirt path right between my sheepskin rug and the windowsill. Hmmm, interesting. The Merkabah card shows a Star Tetrahedron of two interlocking three-sided pyramids spinning in two different directions, and reads: "The frequency* of Merkabah supports our ability to use our consciousness to traverse into other layers of reality and dimensions. It activates our access to our Akashic inheritance as well, merging the totality of our experiences into our present to serve our highest purpose." *Phew, "merging the totality of our experience into our present" definitely sounds like a great idea, with all those different elements in play right now.*

Back on the mountain, the Rock Being beams at me, glowing in the soft sun. And now I also feel the energy of a Merkabah enveloping and gently spinning around me. It feels like it is sheltering me, focusing me, creating presence — distracting or familiar sabotaging thoughts get spun away and never reach its center. The Rock Being, however, *can* apparently join me in the center of the Merkabah. This center looks and feels like I am in the eye of a spinning "storm" and inside a translucent tube that has the same energetic quality as the shield the wizard created around the group of men during the transformation ceremony.

*I am being pulled back into my current reality again. So many things, projects, people, and dreams are vying for my attention — physically, emotionally, and spiritually. Much of it feels deep, multidimensional, intensely transformative, and filled with high frequencies. It's like having my fingers in the socket of life itself — exhilarating, overwhelming, and exhausting at the same time. On another level, I am beginning to understand where it makes sense to find a way to stay very present and at the center of all these centrifugal forces spinning around me in different directions.*

The Rock Being stands very close to me, now, in the center of the Merkabah — too close for comfort, but there isn't much space. It's actually a bit claustrophobic, now that I am paying more attention. *"Can I expand the size of the tube or turn it into a sphere, maybe?"* I wonder. That mere curiosity does the trick. The center turns into a large sphere, which seems like it could be expanded as wide as I would like. The Rock Being now settles into a comfortable distance. It is still quite mysterious, and has not spoken or otherwise communicated with me.

"I communicate with you in your dreams," I hear.

In my dreams.... Well, *this* is a dream, isn't it? And with that contemplation, the Rock Being begins melting, dissolving into the translucent, shimmery shield of the sphere. And I notice how *alive* this shield, this backdrop, is. It is absolutely brimming with the juiciest, most alive ever-changing energy. As I begin to tap into the sheer excitement of it, I still feel peaceful and somehow grounded in lightness at the center of the Merkabah on the very top of the mountain. So if this *is* indeed a dream, it is ok for unusual things to occur, right? My brain relaxes slightly at that thought. Except I *know*, somewhere deep inside, that this isn't actually a dream but a different layer of reality showing itself.

By now, I am somewhat used to going from extraordinary experience to extraordinary experience, and I simply focus on breathing deeply, and on being at the center of the Merkabah and the center of my own energy field.

And the message from before comes floating back into my awareness: "Follow your heart so fully until that is all you know...." I can feel how my heart is opening, expanding wider and wider as I am peacefully breathing, focusing on those words. I can definitely *feel* my heart. It is actually growing in such a way that it's beginning to completely surround me. But how can I follow it? I am "stuck" in the middle of two wildly spinning pyramids on top of the tallest mountain on Earth.

"You are not stuck at all," comes the transmission, the knowing. "'Merkabah' means chariot. You are inside the most powerful vehicle in consciousness."

"So how do I use this vehicle, then?"

I feel like a novice driver who has just been offered a Formula 1 racecar — a bit out of my depth.

"Depth, he-he. It's all about *lightness*," I hear a chuckle from somewhere. It seems like it's vibrating from the shimmery shield, although I cannot quite pinpoint the exact location. "You are good at lightness."

Well, yes, I kind of am. Lightness and ease feel much more like my natural habitat than deep waters, for sure.

"Still, what do I do?" I inquire.

"Ask your heart, it knows!" the shield offers as a sound vibration.

As I ask my heart, it begins to show me scenes that look beautiful and exciting to me — my version of Heaven on Earth. It makes me happy to look at them. My heart opens even more, and all this overflowing love wants to tumble out like a stream of lava creating new land. What a fitting image, as I am still located on top of a volcanic mountain! But I get the sense that instead of going somewhere or leaving that space inside the Merkabah, the Merkabah is drawing, magnetizing to me what I will need to create from the lava of my overflowing love what I can feel and envision as *my* personal Heaven on Earth. Presence and peaceful excitement, coupled with overflowing love. Is that how you ride that powerful chariot?

"There is only one thing missing," I hear. "Gratitude! It's the magic ingredient and ultimate fuel. Gratitude for *all* — past, present, *and* future."

Claudia Sasse

Follow your heart
and keep following it so fully
until that is all you know.

# *9*

---

"Look up at the stars!" comes the transmission.

The sun has set without me even noticing. How could I have missed that? The sunset must have been spectacular from the mountaintop. By now, a canopy of stars has appeared. Wow! I step out of the shelter of the Merkabah and can feel the cold wind in my face. Being out here in the open, alone on the very top of this powerful windy mountain in the middle of the ocean under an indescribably vast and dazzlingly beautiful canopy of stars is intensely frightening and exhilarating at the same time. How very, very tiny I am in this vastness. Yet I feel connected to all — as if a line is being drawn from my heart to every single star out there. Like I am the stars and the stars are me. I am the mountain and the mountain is me. I am the ocean and the ocean is me.

*This scene reminds me of a short story I wrote a few years ago. Am I supposed to share it here? "Yes," comes the simple answer.*

## STARS

The young man was walking along the beach. It was a perfect day — warm, with the sun shining high in the sky. Yet his mood was not reflecting the beautiful scene *at all*. He felt hopeless, and sad, and mad, and abandoned, and treated unfairly. When his dad appeared next to him out of nowhere, he was glad he could finally let this stream of venomous desperation spill out of him. So for the past 30 minutes he had complained, and ranted, and sulked as his dad walked silently next to him, making his presence felt, patiently listening to all of the dark tales flowing like gooey, sticky tar from the lips of his favorite son, dripping onto the sand being hardened by the soft blue water.

After exactly 33 minutes and 33 seconds, the older man put his hand on the boy's back — just a little to the left, on the backside of his heart. He chuckled a little to himself as he found himself playing the "numbers game." *3333* — a number that resonated with encouragement, assistance, freedom, adventure, inspiration, and hope.

Clearly feeling his dad's hand on his back made the young man stop in his tracks. With his gaze still hypnotically focused on the sand, he barely dared breathing, so as not to lose the sensation. Abruptly, he became painfully aware that he must actually be dreaming. His dad had been dead for over three years. He *so* missed him every *single* day — his steady presence, his advice, his unwavering love.

When his dad began to speak, his voice sounded just as calm and confident as the young man remembered. "Look up! What do you see, Son?" Since the young man had been stuck in his anger and sorrow, his head had been hanging low and he had almost blindly been putting one foot in front of the other. Now, for the first time, he allowed his eyes to become unglued from the ground. As he looked up, the scene changed in the blink of an eye, and he saw the most brilliant night sky he had *ever* seen. "I see stars...."

"No," his dad replied, "what do you SEE?"

"I see millions of stars, Dad."

"NO! WHAT DO YOU SEE?" his father's voice taking on a sharper tone.

"I see a sky like I have never seen before, full of lights, stars shining bright."

"You saw the light and not the darkness, right? Do the same in your life!"

And with that the young man woke up from his sleep.

At the same time, the young woman was also *wide* awake. She had gotten up *way* earlier than she had planned, and had driven for over an hour through the pitch black without seeing a single sign of human life (except for that *one* car in the parking lot a few miles below the summit) to watch the sunrise from one of the towering peaks that bordered the vast, deserted valley. The valley was so huge, so seemingly barren, and so far from civilization that you could hear the deafening roar of silence thundering in your ears. She had been to that mountaintop before — during the day. The nearly 6000-foot drop on almost all sides to the bottom of the valley floor had already been disorienting and dizzying then. But at night it looked scary and felt surreal — like she had just entered a different world. One that she inhabited all on her own.

She took a deep breath and opened the door of her van. The cold wind on the wide-open mountain almost took her breath away, and within seconds she was back in the warm shelter of her car, feeling a little safer and more at ease again. She exhaled a sigh of relief — until she realized that what was sheltering her from the blustering winds was also keeping her in a little box away from the wildness and freedom of this majestic mountain under the stars. Mustering all her courage, she bundled up and got out of her car, leaning against the hood, still not entirely ready to leave its familiar protection.

She was thinking about that other car a few miles from her. And this thought terrified her. She was painfully aware how vulnerable she was — exposed to the elements, far from anybody who could help her, while not knowing if there were humans or animals lurking in the dark, ready to attack. Her heart racing, the wind and the altitude keeping her off balance, she was *not* willing to go back and stay in the seeming safety of her car. All she could do was trust. As she took breath after deep breath, facing her fears yet not backing down, they began subsiding, almost like they were done playing their role. And eventually, they walked offstage.

She lifted her head and looked at the sky. In the moonless night, the stars were more brilliant than she had ever seen them. There were millions and millions of them, almost close enough to reach. The experience was indescribable. She felt alive as never before, present, exhilarated, filled with overflowing gratitude. She felt like she had found HER place among all of these stars.

And then a thought crossed her mind that made her briefly sad. She was all alone up here. This seemed to be HER mountaintop. What if life really *was* lonely at the top? And then the stars began whispering their answer: "Life does not have to be lonely at the top. We are all connected through our hearts. With that connection, we weave a net of love with each other. Only those with an open heart who are connected to the brilliance of their own light will recognize these deep, light-filled, powerful connections."

With that, she opened her arms and her heart as wide as she could, and she danced and twirled under the brilliant blanket of stars until she felt like she almost lifted off to fly and dance in the sky with the wild wind.

When the young woman and the young man finally met, both of them carried the knowing of their own light and brilliance within them. Somehow, they did something that they had never done with another person before: They fearlessly opened their hearts, recognizing each other's brilliance with the core of their being, igniting a bond of light that could never be broken, allowing each other to shine more brightly than ever before. As their light kept growing and expanding, they began noticing others around them brilliantly growing their light, as well. As they *all* began fearlessly connecting their hearts, they found themselves weaving the most beautiful tapestry of peace, light, and love — growing a new garden of joy, play, fun, and overflowing gratitude *together*.

Look up! What do you see?

# 10

"I want it ALL!" has been flowing through my awareness, popping in, pulling at my clothes, jumping up and down in front of my face like a little kid trying to get my attention. I want it ALL! And what does ALL even mean to me? Maybe I am afraid to even look at that. What if I declare what that means to me and it'll never happen, or is way too hard to "achieve"?

"Rich" was the word that summarized it all when I went up to be with Mauna Kea last night. I had been invited into a communion with this powerful mountain — just for me. Being with the mountain, feeling like I was melting into the mountain, hearing its welcoming motherly voice, hiking up to the sanctuary of the summit, watching the sunset glow red across the valley and light up the mountainside, and then gazing at the awe-inspiring light show of the stars from a vortex field at the side of the mountain. It was the incredible, heart-opening experience of living a physical version of what I have been writing about. And at the end of the night, the word I walked away with, the word for my life here on Earth going forward, was "RICH." Rich in every sense of the meaning: colorful, multifaceted, full-on, vajayjay-tingling, multidimensional, abundant, real juicy richness.

Now, I was not born rich. And presently, I am anything but rich in the classical sense. Instead, I am really good at "making do," making things that are ok-ish very practical, fun, and magical. That's what I grew up with; that's what I know.

But now we are talking about painting with a full-color palette. It should be exciting, right? Except it feels scary. I have no idea how to do that, or where to even get the paint. And what if I don't like what I paint? And still, the words "Rich" and "I want it ALL!" are ringing in my ears, becoming louder *and louder, and making me smile :) And I recognize that this beautiful island I get to live on is rich, overflowing, incredibly alive, juicy, and abundant.*

*As I write these words, I'm sitting not on my usual sheepskin rug but at the dining table of a gorgeously designed, modern, wide-open house with sweeping views of Maui — a house I would have picked for myself. The environment feels rich, spacious, clear — like Breathing Spaces, the name of my company and of the retreat space I'll be creating. Wow! Grateful!*

"Where I have been, no one will go!" I remember those words ... and have to smile. "Laura?" I ask, looking around.

"Here! I am here!"

Laura comes running towards me, waving both arms, laughing, a little out of breath, as she is so often. I have to laugh, too. I'm really happy to see her. As I look around, I notice that we are on the slopes of a bright, almost electrifyingly green grassy hill — juicy, vibrant, brimming with life. The sun is shining brightly, the birds are chirping enthusiastically. Spring, rebirth — 1001 possibilities.

"OMG, I have to show you something. Come, come, come!" Laura grabs my hand and pulls me along, half-skipping, half-running.

Still laughing, I fall into step with her. I have no clue where we are headed, but I can *feel* her excitement — the juiciness of what she wants to show me. "Juicy" — there's that word again... :)

"I have to change my entry phrase," Laura exclaims suddenly. "It's not true anymore, 'Where I have been, no one will go!' Where I have been, you *can* go, now. And I am *so* very excited!"

After about five minutes of running and my growing anticipation, we come to a sudden stop — fortunately!!! Because we are at a cliff — a deep chasm gaping before us.

"Whoa, Laura!" I say out loud, silently adding, "Are you crazy?"

I scramble to catch my balance, feeling like I almost went over the edge. Once I'm halfway recovered from the shock, I notice that the place reminds me a little of a cliff-side I know in Switzerland.

"Apparently you are finding it very exciting to almost kill me!" I am still quite angry at Laura, but I can't help feeling this utter juicy excitement. "Will you enlighten me what this is about?"

Obligingly, she says, "See?" and points at a little chapel perched on the edge of a steep rocky drop-off across the chasm. "I made that for you."

"Um, you made that for me? Why would I need a chapel on the side of a cliff on the other side of a steep canyon?"

"You can put your prayers there, your treasures, your wishes, your secret dreams. It can hold them all. Inside, it is as big as you need it to be. It can hold whole universes." Laura looks at me with bright beaming eyes, as if all this should be obvious to me.

I try to wrap my brain around this.

"Not your brain, your heart," Laura says, reading my thoughts and commanding me: "Wrap your heart around it!"

"Laura," I answer, trying my hardest not to be impatient, "what is the point of storing my biggest dreams in a little treasure chapel on a cliff that I cannot even reach without either killing myself or attempting a very arduous and unsafe climb down this mountain and up the opposite side?"

I am not getting it… and I am annoyed, seriously annoyed. Laura smiles a sweet, loving, soft-pink-fluffy-jacket kind of smile and puts one arm around my shoulders. "Come, let's sit down here for a minute."

I sit next to her on the thick grass dotted with sweet little yellow flowers. Her sweetness has taken away my thunder, and I am not mad anymore, just exhausted.

I take a few deep breaths, and feel how I am coming back into balance. I can still feel a bit of the excitement, but it isn't overpowering anymore. I feel more peaceful, now. Laura speaks, but her voice — instead of sounding next to me — seems to reach me from the chapel across the canyon.

"What you think of as a 'great divide' can be merely a tiny step over the smallest of cracks. Do you remember the little Rock Being hiding behind the cairn and how, for a split second, you perceived the small cairn as a big tower? This situation is the same. If you change your perspective, the chapel is right here in front of you. And to answer the question that you are about to ask, it *is* a chapel, because your dreams, wishes, and desires are sacred and need to be held in a sacred container. Go ahead, go inside and see what your dream world looks and feels like."

Ok, so I simply need to change my perspective and just take a small step to arrive at the front door of the chapel? I still see nothing but a gaping chasm in front of me, but I somehow trust Laura….

*"BREATHE — LET GO — TRUST" shoots through my head — the words that are hanging on my bathroom wall, written across a photo of a chapel on the side of a cliff in Switzerland….*

I get up from my seat on the grass, take a deep breath, close my eyes, and step forward off the cliff. Yet instead of free-falling through the air, I experience my foot bouncing on the soft grass outside the white steepled building. Wow, I made it! I actually made it!

Laura is standing right there, by my side, and gives me the biggest hug. "I know how much courage and trust that took," she says. "Are you ready to go in?"

I am surprised how my apprehension has vanished after stepping over the canyon, and I am actually feeling an excited anticipation and, somehow, gratitude. I am grateful for all the

Claudia Sasse

choices I made to get to this point. Grateful that I am actually daring to really take a look at my dreams for the first time in my life. Grateful to Laura for bringing me here.

"Yes, Laura," I announce, smiling from ear to ear, "let's go!"

But she surprises me by saying — very lovingly and almost with reverence — "No, sweetheart, this is for you to enter on your own."

# DREAM WITH ME

Spun out of rainbow crystal and gold
Gossamer threads softly reaching out from our hearts
Delicate, magical, powerful
Strength rooted in light
Threads finding each other
Weaving together in a graceful dance
Of love and creation
Knowing Heaven
Walking on Earth
Building a Home
Creating a HEARTH

# 11

I take a deep breath and walk towards the door of the chapel. It is a roughhewn construction made out of dark wood, but as I get closer it changes to the shimmery translucency of the shield that I already know from the circle of men during the forgiveness ceremony and the Merkabah. I wonder if I can simply walk through the shield, and when I try, there is no resistance. It actually feels like a warm and welcoming hug.

As I enter the chapel, I have the odd sensation of walking directly into my own heart. Bright white light streams into a wide-open space. The air feels clear, crisp, refreshing, caressed by a gentle breeze — a clear space of love. I feel at home here, light, buoyant, magical — yes, magical. As if I should be holding a sparkly wand and twirling inside a spiral of fairy dust.

So where are my dreams? Where are my wishes? Where are my desires? Are they *already* here, or do I have to somehow *place* them here? I see a man walking — more like floating on air — towards me. Matching the space, he is dressed all in white, like an angel. There is *definitely* something angelic about him....

Actually, now that I am paying more attention, there are thousands and thousands of angelic beings appearing in multiple circles all around me. Each is holding out a gift. Some of the gifts are wrapped in white, others in all kinds of beautiful colors. And all with a ribbon and bow.

The floating angel seems to be a "tour guide" of sorts. Though he doesn't really speak, he must be transmitting something. Because out of nowhere, I know that all these gifts I see are my dreams, wishes and desires. Some, I came to Earth with. Others, I have developed through being here and living my life. Some are dreams I share with other people.

The colorful ones are those that are ready to be activated and brought into physical existence/experience. Activating them is apparently much like unwrapping Christmas gifts.

All these gifts are *for* me, selected *by* me, actually. Some of them require a bit of assembly, while others are already perfect, beautiful treasures just as they are. And some are meant to be enjoyed together with other people.

Still, the assembly part concerns me a bit, as well as how to know which present to unwrap first. Ah, apparently, the angels are there to help with the assembly, if required. Sweet!

And which present is first?

"Just follow your knowing," I hear.

A thought crosses my mind: Why are all my dreams and desires wrapped? Am I hiding them from myself? But apparently (the angels let me know), it's so I don't become overwhelmed with the sheer magnitude of it all, and so I can enjoy and really be present with each one.

*Being present with a present.…. :) What if being present IS the present? I muse.*

I slowly turn in a circle, smiling, feeling grateful for each angelic being so patiently holding out my gifts. And then my attention gets drawn to a beautiful, shiny, bright-pink box with purple dots and a green bow that an angel in the second circle row is holding out to me. I wonder if he could possibly meet me in the center, so I can take a closer look. And before I can even finish the thought, he is right in front of me, smiling warmly, holding out the box towards me.

Nodding and smiling in grateful acknowledgment, I take the box out of his hands, untie the bow, and take off the lid. As if I have just freed the genie from the bottle, a beautiful scene unfolds all around me. I find myself transported to a lush hillside with sweeping ocean views.

Claudia Sasse

Cows are grazing below. I hear water running nearby, and a big tree is inviting me to visit it. The land feels rich and abundant. It is telling a story, the story of creation itself. I feel cradled by this land, welcomed like a long-lost daughter. It is sanctuary and wilderness. The soil is fertile and rich. You can grow beautiful organic food here. Another layer of the vision appears, and the land looks partially transformed. There are people in the picture now, some of them farming. I can see a prolific vegetable garden, sheep, goats, a pond, a sweet little wooden house with a beautiful deck near the pond. The people I see walking the grounds seem happy, smiling — each fulfilling a task that lights them up, their part of the puzzle. Above, higher up towards the sky, is a cluster of small houses and a large octagonal pavilion — a retreat space. People here seem to be enjoying the peacefulness and power of the land and the retreat space.

So what is *my* role in all this? Certainly, I am not a farmer. I seem to be more a steward of the space — opening it up to people from all walks of life, all kinds of cultures to come together . . . helping to preserve the land's heritage and nature, as well as allowing for new possibilities and collaborative projects to emerge.

*My own story is truly being interwoven within the story of the book, right now. The very first morning I came to the Big Island of Hawaii, I became aware of a huge 485-acre parcel of land. I have never stepped foot on it, but my eyes get drawn to it whenever I drive by on my way to Pololū Valley. I hadn't thought about the fact that it is still for sale. I certainly don't own the 3.2 million dollars that it's listed for. Neither do I have the means or the faintest clue how to build a retreat and begin farming the land. And still. . . .*

*With growing intensity, I find that this is all very much in my awareness right now. And I am here to create a retreat, aren't I? And what I am to create has always felt so much bigger than "just" a retreat. Yes, it would start as a Women's Retreat, and that might always be at the core of it.*

*But ultimately, it would be an incubator and support system for new ideas and businesses. A place for people, leaders from all over the world, to come together and get to know each other — meet as fellow humans, explore peaceful solutions for the world's many problems, support each other, collaborate, and celebrate together.*

My heart is racing. Whoa, is this truly the first dream for me to unpack? It is huge, crazy, way beyond my current capacities, I'm thinking. And still . . . when I take a moment and simply breathe and feel into it, I can feel my heart smiling and laughing, jumping up and down with glee and excitement. YES! I want this.

As I begin to think about all the "why not's" and potential difficulties, I hear: "There will be help. You are there to illuminate the space."

But how would I even get people there?

And again: "There will be help. You are there to illuminate the space. Yes, your dreams *can* come true, and they can come true miraculously and with so much joy and ease. You would not have been given a dream like this if it weren't for you to realize."

Angels or no, I find myself protesting, "But what if I immerse myself in a project like that and don't like it? You all gotta know how much I value my freedom!"

"This *is* your freedom," I hear. "*Your* way to fully and creatively express yourself. This is your home."

Claudia Sasse

# CONNECTED

So often, we have moments in our lives where we feel alone and separate — like we have to figure it all out by ourselves.

Yet what if we were on an adventure *with* each other? Hearts melting into each other. Profoundly experiencing the depth of each other and our environment. Being inspired to new heights of expansion by what we are immersed in at the moment.

What if we can feel this connection regardless if we are with one person, thousands, or even millions? It's like our hearts beat as one.

And we have seen versions of this in action before. It united a people to fight for their right of domination as the "chosen" race, just to spread death and devastation in the world, as in Nazi Germany. It has united a race in their fight for equality led by Martin Luther King, Jr.

What if *this* version (vision) will unite *all* the people on our planet? What if *this* time, it is not about fighting, but instead about deeply connecting our hearts in the infinite colorful creation of more beauty, love, growth, expansion, and light, with respect and admiration for everyone involved? Our hearts beating as one, until the sound becomes thunderous as it echoes and reverberates across the Universe, powerfully sending out a signal that irresistibly attracts other beings/life forms of the same vibration, to create an even greater web of connection across galaxies . . . as we become fractals* in this ever-expanding experience, beyond comprehension, born out of love, compassion, and conscious connections.

Each of us becoming our own Universe within ourselves of deep self-love, compassion, and deep connection to ourselves. Thundering out into other Universes in its reverberation. Every cell, every atom in our bodies vibrating at the same rate as we dive deeper and deeper into ourselves.

I see each and every one of us being fully grounded in the wholeness of our being. As we freely share our gifts, we get to explore, play, create, and expand together. We don't complete each other, as each and every one of us is already whole and complete within ourselves. We complement and enhance each other.

*Fractal: a geometrical or physical structure having an irregular or fragmented shape at all scales of measurement between a greatest and *smallest scale*

## CONNECTED VIDEO

https://tinyurl.com/Video-Connected

Claudia Sasse

# *12*

---

*GRATITUDE!!!* The word rings in my ears, appearing in front of me like a Las Vegas neon sign. I feel it deeply, absorbing it with each one of my senses. Gratitude — the secret ingredient to activate the true power of the Merkabah....

Still immersed in the vision of the dream that I just opened up, I wonder why — all of a sudden — gratitude is all around me with such an intensity. It almost feels like I am being rewired to default to gratitude.

Hmmm... when I first received the vision of my dream, I went into thinking about its potential challenges and problems pretty quickly. Is this my autopilot, then — going into the problem side of things — examining why my dreams couldn't work out, or why I wouldn't even *want* them to work out? That would sure put a brake on anything, wouldn't it — even a Merkabah?

But the gratitude that I am flooded with feels soft, heart-opening, and allowing. It says YES to *all* that life is offering — YES to receiving it with love — YES to being grateful for all the different options. And I have the impression that while receiving all in gratitude, I can still have the freedom to choose what I like the most.

Two angels come float-walking towards me, smiling sweetly, albeit a bit mischievously (who knew that angels could be mischievous?). They position themselves on either side of me, facing the other direction, and link arms with me. The next thing I know, we are airborne. I am being lifted up and flown...I have no idea where. I can see a blue sky with perfect white fluffy clouds, but because I am facing backwards I can only see the chapel and the mountainside where we just came from. Gravity should be pulling my body to the ground, and this whole arrangement should feel highly unsafe and scary — except that it doesn't. I feel light as a feather (an angel feather?). As a matter of fact, it feels like the two angels and I are one unit, so that I can't fall. So I decide to simply relax and enjoy the ride.

"Thank you for gifting me this book to write." *I silently express my gratitude to no one in particular, but to the loving energy flowing through me as I am writing — being fed words, images, ideas, feelings, and energies to weave into this story. It feels like a seemingly simple yet rich multidimensional tapestry, with more and more facets and layers revealing themselves whenever I reread what I have written.*

Gratitude! Can I be grateful for this angel ride, despite the fact that it feels slightly crazy and I have no idea where we are going? I actually can. This is unlike any experience I have ever had before. I can trust these angels :).

Wait, wait! How do I *know* that I can trust these angels? They *did* look mischievous, didn't they? You wouldn't expect mischief from angels, right?

With that thought, the weather changes. Ominous dark clouds roll in, and a cold wind starts whipping around us, instantly freezing me to the core. Big raindrops begin to splash down, and the electricity of a lightning storm makes the hair on my arms stand up.

On top of that, I don't feel light, safe, and secure anymore. I am getting heavier by the second, the rain soaks my clothes, and I notice how I am beginning to slip out of the angels' arm hold.

"OMG, STOP!!" I scream at the top of my lungs, fearing for my life, now.

And we actually do stop. We come to a halt right away. The angels gently set me down on top of a very barren, very rocky needle-point of a mountaintop with steep cliffs all around us. I am FURIOUS.

Claudia Sasse

"What the f$%@ are you guys thinking? Are you trying to kill me? How the hell are we going to get down from here? Obviously, that 'flying' thing is not an option."

The angels just stand there, smiling peacefully. Peacefully? WTF! I am scared. I am freezing. I feel utterly alone. Actually, worse than alone — on top of the scariest mountain ever with two whacked-out, peacefully smiling angels (or whatever those guys are supposed to be).

I try to breathe through my panic and collect my thoughts, which is almost impossible in the pounding rain and freezing wind. The electricity of a thunderstorm is making my hairs stand up as I see flashes of lightning hitting the mountain next to us. And then, as if one of the bolts of lightning that I am hypnotically staring at ignites my brain and connects the dots, I remember the Merkabah — being on top of a mountain in the shelter of the Merkabah with everything else spinning around me in all kinds of directions. The Merkabah is a vehicle, right? So I *should* be able to get off this scary rock. Except I have to do it very quickly, as the lightning storm is beginning to move even closer.

Ok, ok, I close my eyes and take a deep breath, trying to concentrate. What are the pieces needed to ride this chariot again? *Presence* is one. Oh God, I so don't want to be present right now. I want to be just about *anywhere* else than here. But if this is my only way out, I'd better get with it.

*It's quite ironic that it feels almost impossible to stay present with this. I am feeling incredibly distracted, my thoughts and feelings going all over the place. What is so dang scary about simply being present?*

It feels almost impossible, but I tell myself to breathe deeply and simply be with the situation without needing to change it, any of it. And I sit down, rain pouring all around me, while the angels stand there quietly watching. I ignore them and actually begin feeling a bit calmer. After a few moments I even remember the power of opening my heart, and I deliberately direct my breath there. Despite the storm raging around me, it feels peaceful when I concentrate on my heart. And I notice how the shimmery shield of the Merkabah center creates itself around me, little by little. I stay with it, breathing calmly into my heart, focusing on nothing else.

And the oddest thing happens, in the middle of the probably worst, most life-threatening situation of my life: All I can feel is overwhelming love, my heart literally bursting open, overflowing. Why? What for? I have no idea. It seems non-specific — a pure kind of love for all that is.

I am so focused on this beautiful way of being that I do not even notice, at first, that the shield of the Merkabah has completed itself, and I am sitting in a dry, perfectly tempered spot now. I can even see the sun breaking through the clouds. Gratitude washes over me. I know that all my problems have not been solved. I am still precariously perched on the steepest mountain ever; but I am so incredibly grateful for the love that I am feeling and that's pouring out of me, and the fact that I am now in a dry, warm, and increasingly sunny place, shielded from any storm that might come my way. *This* seems more important than any problem I might still be facing, and I am not willing to leave this space. A calm, sweet peacefulness settles over me as I stay with that energy.

And then I can feel this little bit of excitement bubbling up. Excitement about what? I close my eyes and notice how I am excited and grateful about my journey — all of it — what was, what is, and what is to come. Like I am anticipating great things and am grateful in advance, which seems a crazy notion while sitting on a scary mountain with no idea how to get down from here. And still, it feels like the most beautiful and natural thing to do, somehow. So I am sitting inside the shield with the Merkabah now spinning around me, my eyes closed, with a big grin plastered across my face.

Claudia Sasse

A thought lazily wafts in after a while: "*Maybe it's time to figure out how to get back to life, civilization, other humans.*"

When I open my eyes for a second, I immediately shut them again, shake my head, and rub them a little. When I open them again, the scene that I see is still the same. I am not on a scary mountaintop anymore, but on a tree-lined strip of grass — an avenue that leads directly towards a big castle. HOLY sh*%!! The Merkabah! It worked!!!

I am stunned, speechless, just staring at the castle, when I see the two angels float-walking up to me, smiling warmly.

"That was a hard lesson, and we are so very proud of you," they transmit. "Will you join us? We want to show you something."

Gratitude flooding in
Sweet, abundant, powerful
Overflowing
Why?
It doesn't matter
I am dancing in love with an old friend

## 13

*And there it is again, the gratitude to be able to write this story. The written word allowing me to express truth — my truth — in a deeper way than through conversations alone. My truth…*

*Even though I feel like I am being gifted with this story, it also feels like I am sharing my truth. And if this is MY truth, is there a universal truth where we all connect? And if so, am I accessing it with these writings?*

We are heading towards the castle, white with purple accents, like the picture in my favorite Memory game — that kid's game of matching pairs — has come to life. A flag is being raised on its roof, which — if I remember correctly — means that the king or queen is just arriving home. A castle, home to the sovereign, house of wealth, subject of dreams and fairytales, placeholder for possibilities, supported by many, supporting many.

Somehow, I feel turned on — by the fullness of life, by the new expanded possibilities that I can sense all around me, by the bigger world that is opening up in front of me. The sheer magnitude of what seems to be coming at me, circling around me, and flowing through me like a fierce wind, is so immense that I am almost tempted to turn around and head the other way. Except I don't. I lean into the wind, looking left and right to make sure I still have the angels by my side. Now that I understand the experience they helped create for me to truly know the power of the Merkabah, I know they are here to support my journey, and I am really grateful for their presence.

"Are you nervous?" one of them transmits.

Hmmm, I guess I am. I don't quite know why, as I have no idea why we are headed towards the castle. Somehow, I feel I am supposed to be there. I am invited — the guest of honor, even. But what if I am not good enough for the castle? What if I will behave incorrectly, wear the wrong clothes, am not smart or educated enough to have an intelligent conversation? What if everyone, including me, finds out that I am really a fraud, not in integrity, not truthful, not fit to be honored, or even *be* in the castle, however briefly that might be?

The angels move in front of me, blocking the fierceness of the wind. This makes me feel cared for and protected, but — truth be told — I kind of *like* wind. The phrase *"The Winds of Change"* will often float through my head. Wind makes me feel buoyant, exhilarated, and free. Only sometimes, it is too much — when I'm not sure of myself, when I'm a bit afraid, when I don't feel strong or good enough.

We arrive at the gate. There is a wrought-iron-and-golden fence around the perimeter of the castle, but the gate is wide open, inviting, no guards to be seen. It is a beautiful, peaceful summer afternoon. The sun warms the small round pebbles of the white gravel inside the fence. The humming of bees is in the air. I wonder where their flowers are — maybe on the backside of the castle?

We walk around the perimeter to the back, the white gravel softly crunching under my feet.

The backside opens up to the expanse of a beautifully cared-for lawn, dotted and framed by tall, mature trees. There are patches of flowers all over, many looking like delicate yet robust wildflowers. The landscaping seems like a mixture of a wild, natural environment, and the carefully planned and manicured spaces one might expect from a typical castle garden.

On the lawn, people are playing or sitting at small tables. Some look human, while others look more like my angel friends. What they have in common is, that they are all dressed in white. Those at the tables have tall glasses of what seems to be iced tea or sparkling water, decorated with sprigs of mint or edible flowers. The scene is joyful, peaceful. The people within it appear to be moving at random, and yet it feels like they are playing their perfect part within the whole picture. Like the dancing flight of the bees.

A man who looks like a butler (white gloves and all) comes towards us across the lawn, smiling, with both arms outstretched.

"You're here!" he exclaims. "Come! We have been waiting for you, Dear One." And before I can even think or say, "For me???!!" he claps his white-gloved hands. Oddly enough, this causes a very loud, deeply resonant sound that catches everyone's attention. It must be audible even in the furthest reaches of the gardens, because immediately the people all turn towards our little group standing by the entrance, and smile, cheer, and clap their hands.

The butler gently nudges me forward. "Speak to them!" he invites me, kindly but firmly, and I can't help feeling that I don't really have much of an option. "Tell them your truth!"

"Wait, what?" I exclaim. "What am I supposed to tell them, and why?" I am so confused, scared, and ashamed at the same time. Who are those people? What do they want from me? They all look beautiful and perfectly at home in this setting, while I just came from a rain-drenched, freezing mountaintop. I probably look like a dirty, wet cat. It hadn't even occurred to me to do anything about my appearance before we set off for the castle. There probably are streaks of mascara running down my face.

"Tell them your truth!" the gentle command comes again.

I can see a sea of eager faces turned towards me, smiling in anticipation. And then the sun illuminates only the spot I am standing on and dims around everyone else, as if we are in a theater. It's an odd sensation, having the sun as a spotlight. It's probably painfully highlighting every flaw I have while everybody looks at me to give them something — and I don't really know what that "something" is. And then all that fades from my awareness, as if the sun spotlight is shining not only *on* me but also *into* me, focusing my own attention on my heart. My truth lives in my heart, right?

I take a deep breath, as I have done so often these days, and just stand there in the outer spotlight. I close my eyes, place my hands on my chest, follow my inner spotlight, and connect to my heart — listening, observing, feeling, wondering what wants to be said. After a moment, I can feel the by-now somewhat familiar sensation of my heart opening, expanding. Love is flowing, swirling through me at a rapid rate; and when I feel that it's beginning to overflow, I open my mouth, not knowing what words will come out.

"Beloveds," I find myself saying, "I am beyond grateful that I get to be with you today. I can feel the absolute pure beauty of your hearts — of every single one of your hearts. The magnitude of this is enormous. It literally brings me to tears. While I don't exactly know why we are gathered here, I can feel the incredible power of our hearts, our pure essence weaving together. I can see how all of our hearts are being ignited. We can shine. It is safe to shine. There really IS only love. Will you breathe that in with me for a moment? Will you breathe into the beauty and purity of your own heart *and* into the love that connects us all? Will you dare to feel this with me for a moment? Let's just be here now like this. Just for now. It is safe to do this in this moment, while we are here together."

Except that as I am talking about this being all safe, I abruptly sense dark thunderclouds, like those on the mountain, looming at the periphery of the large castle garden. Surely, the people on the edges will get drenched in a second. I still remember how awful it was on the mountaintop, and I want to warn them. Maybe it is *not* safe here in this moment, after all. Somehow, I feel responsible for the wellbeing and safety of these people.

As I contemplate all this, it seems as if the sun above my head is beginning to dim ever so slightly. But what I notice is that other people in various places in the gardens have their own spotlight in the sun, by now, creating warm circles around them — a safe place from the looming thunderstorm. And people begin forming little clusters around them in the shelter of their warmth and light.

What happens next is astounding. One by one, all the others ignite their own spotlight, their own sun. The power of this literally melts the ominous clouds, until what is left is a beautiful, sunny summer afternoon. Except that the scene feels different from the one I first walked into. Now, people feel ignited, purposeful, empowered, and deeply connected with each other.

*What about the angels*, I wonder? I'd seen many of them on the lawn, initially, but afterwards they completely slipped out of my awareness.

I hear the transmission: "We are very honored to be able to assist your transformation, but we are not actively part of it."

# I See You

https://tinyurl.com/I-See-You-Love

# 14

What wants to be said next? I wonder. Is there anything to be said? People seem to be happily lit up and clustered in their groups. So I just stand there for a moment in deep gratitude, receiving all of their beautiful light — and my own. I notice how I need to expand somehow to make room for it all. But as I relax into breathing it all in, this expansion seems to happen naturally.

It occurs to me that although I actually don't have a microphone, everyone in the castle garden looks like they have heard me. "They heard you because you spoke from your heart," the butler tells me, stepping closer and smiling warmly. "Remember to do this, always, and people will hear you. I know you feel like you have not properly ended your speech, but the people here also feel your enormous gratitude for them right now, and that is enough."

"So... what do we do now?" I inquire. "And whose castle is this? Where is the sovereign? The sovereign should be here, since the flags are raised — right?" He smiles again with this incredible warmth, which appears very un-butler-like to me, and guides me to a little white wrought-iron table on the side of the garden, in the shelter of a few bushes. It almost feels like I am offstage in a dressing room, now — except there are no mirrors, make-up, or dresses, only nature and a tall glass with a clear iced drink and mint in it.

"This is your castle. You are the sovereign." The butler looks at me intently and very lovingly at the same time.

It seems impossible to stay with the story. My mind is wandering all over the place. I have somehow been suspecting this information, but I have no idea what to do with it. I keep *zoning out, almost like I don't want to actually know what is going to be channeled through, next. Almost like I am afraid of the truth.*

I digest this information. It is too enormous to even go, "*Huh?*" Yet at the same time, it's as if I knew it all along. So I just sit very still, almost wary not to move so as not to cause ripples in the wrong way.

"And how do I...?" I start. But even that, I know.

I govern this place (or *from* this place) through my heart — and through play. Interesting... play. Yet there is no other way to move, motivate, or change anything or anybody here. And I guess I'd also have to be clear — very clear.

Why is this so terrifying? It should be easy, light, fun, a skip and a hop through the castle gardens. They are *my* castle gardens, after all. I am allowing the discomfort, the terror, to be there. If I am the sovereign of this place, then I really don't have anybody else to hand this off to. And I also know that I need to be patient and compassionate with myself. So I soften into that. I always thought I had my smallish kind of life to figure out, not a whole castle.

It occurs to me to ask the angels for assistance. Maybe they can help. I haven't even finished that thought when not only do my friends from the mountaintop arrive, but so do many other ones who appear around me. The bushes give way to accommodate them.

However, since I don't even know what to ask for, I simply signal, "*Help!*" And then I am flooded with a warm, loving sweetness. I feel cared for — just like when we all were walking through the wind, up to the castle. This somehow gives me the space to be with all this information in a way that doesn't feel overwhelming. I also sense other beings around me — earth beings, fairies, beings of the light realm.... The more I tap into it, the more I can feel this loving, feather-light spaciousness being created around me.

And instead of focusing on the magnitude, the responsibility, the overwhelm, and the idea of not being up to the task, I begin actually feeling the sizzle of the opportunities, the play, the ease, the lightness, the fun, and the sheer giddy joy of it all. And I know that a big silly grin must be appearing on my face. And I *don't* have to do it all by myself. I have support, lots of support.

So I go where I've learned to go recently, and dive into the spaciousness of my heart. I ask it, "What do you want to create here? What would light you up the most?"

Geez, why on earth are those thunderclouds rolling into my field again? Really? I'm getting slightly annoyed and immediately very much pulled out of the heart space. Was that the wrong question? Maybe I am not even supposed to ask questions? "All right guys, help me out here!"

It's the butler who chimes in, "Be present with what is here first, before you put any pressure on yourself to create anything. This *is* already your creation. *Enjoy* it! Give yourself some gratitude for what you have done already. Acknowledge your own brilliance, light, and ability. You are at the perfect place at the perfect time. It cannot be any other way.

So enjoy, celebrate, bask in the light. You just took a major step as a sovereign when you shared your truth with all those people in the most beautiful and powerful way. Let that sink in. Breathe into that. Allow your expansion to happen as you relax into this new space. Whatever you will want to do next will arise naturally. It will bubble up, inspired by your overflow and what those beautiful people will share with you when you talk to them. These conversations will open new possibilities and spark new ideas. But for now, it is time to mingle, connect, and celebrate. You are *so* loved. Your people are waiting for you."

"YES!!"

I can do this. I *want* to meet all these beautiful people who I don't really know yet, but whose hearts I have felt and am already deeply connected with. I *want* to know who they are.

What their lives are like. What their dreams are. Maybe I can support them with that. Maybe *that* is how I serve as sovereign of this place.

I am feeling a sweet kind of anticipation flowing through me as I breathe in the fragrant summer air, feel the sunshine warming and illuminating my skin, and hear the symphonic sound of the bees, the birds, and the breeze ruffling the foliage around me.

Meet me in the stillness of our heart
Meet me in the innocence, the clarity, the purity of our heart
Meet me in the quiet abundance of our heart
Meet me in the unbridled joy of our heart
Meet me in the depth and eternal expansion of our heart
Diving deep while flying high and wild and free
Meet me here

# 15

"Laura!!!" I see her striding across the lawn, and I jump up from my chair and run towards her. "I am *so* happy you're here!"

We hug each other tightly for a long while, feeling our love for each other and immense gratitude for being in each other's presence. I want to blurt out all of my latest adventures, but I know that she already knows. All at once, I become aware that I am still wearing her fluffy pink jacket and I want to give it back to her.

"Keep it for now," she smiles with a twinkle in her eyes, "until you have your own wardrobe that makes you feel cared for and alive and happy and beautiful — clothes that enhance your sparkle."

I have no idea *when* I'll actually get clothes like that, but my inner little girl really likes the sound of it and is jumping up and down with glee and excitement.

"YES! That's what I want my clothes to feel like!"

I had almost forgotten that I probably still looked like a wet cat. When I connected so deeply with all the people on the lawn, that didn't seem to matter so much anymore. But I cannot deny that the thought of new clothes makes me really happy.

And then a thought crosses my mind that makes me feel a bit shallow. "After all these deeply transformational, heart-opening experiences, isn't it quite superficial for me to be concerned with clothes and appearances?" I express it out loud to Laura

"Your body is a work of art and beauty," Laura explains lovingly. "It radiates and transmits who you are into the space around you. If you think about it, your heart is part of your body. In this world, we wear clothing — initially as protection from the weather, but now also as a behavior that most humans have agreed upon, feel most comfortable with, and even feel connected through. So, what if your clothes could be a visible outward expression of your inner heart light, and at the same time hug your body from the outside in a way that allows you to feel loved on the inside — the way you feel my love when you wear my pink jacket?"

Just the sound of that makes me feel beautiful. I close my eyes and relax into that idea. I can feel its alignment, how it settles around me like Laura's jacket, and at the same time I somehow feel undeserving. Where on earth is that coming from?

"Come," Laura says. "I want to show you a part of this place that you haven't been able to see yet."

She pulls me deeper into the left side of the gardens, until we come to a tall hedge of dark green foliage and fragrant white flowers that look like a cross between jasmine and gardenias.

"Star roses…," I muse.

The hedge must be at least seven feet tall. A tall, sturdy, wooden door allows entry, but it only has a small window through which to look in or out. It almost reminds me of an old monastery door. The place looks sweet, yet secretive — open only to those who are invited and carefully vetted.

"Open the door," Laura instructs.

Only now do I notice that there is no door handle. "How can I open it?" I ask.

"Everything will be given," the answer reflects back from the door, as a handle appears in front of my eyes.

*"Everything will be given" was an insight a friend once shared with me after a very deep spiritual journey. This sentence has stuck with me ever since, and I have noticed how all the important things in my life have appeared seemingly*

Claudia Sasse

*out of nowhere and with no effort on my part. All I needed to do was say YES.*

I press down on the handle, and the door swings open with unexpected ease. What I see when I step through it takes my breath away: a sea of flowers in all colors, shapes, and sizes. It could almost be blindingly dazzling in their bright display, but instead it simply feels sweet and precious. Hundreds of butterflies are dancing through the warm summer air, like flowers that have taken flight. This place feels intimate and endless at the same time. There is a white gazebo appearing and disappearing, and then appearing again, in the middle of all the flowers. To the right I see a small stream with a little waterfall happily tumbling over big, round rocks.

"Where are we? What is this?" I ask Laura. I feel her stepping through the door behind me, but I'm not willing to take my eyes off the beauty all around me.

"This is your Secret Garden," she replies with a voice like liquid sunshine.

*My* Secret Garden…. It feels like the flowers are talking to me, sharing their joy, their love, their sweetness, their beauty, and whispering their secrets. I soak it all in. Except, why did I not know about my own secret garden? I guess in the same way I did not know about my own castle. I dismiss the thought.

"This is amazing, Laura," I say, almost in reverence.

"Yes, it really is," she answers, with a smile in her voice. "Everybody's Secret Garden is different and very special in its own way. And I love yours. It feels so sweet, inviting, and inclusive."

"So what is this place about?" I wonder out loud.

Laura steps around me and pulls me towards the gazebo, which is visible in that moment.

"Can we go sit by the waterfall instead of inside the gazebo?" I ask. And the gazebo vanishes again. There is a break in the sea of flowers, and a band of dappled leafy trees border the stream and the waterfall. Somehow, I feel overwhelmed again (as so often happens, these days) and want to be close to the strong steadiness of the trees and the cool, cleansing gurgling of the water flowing around the rocks.

Actually, I feel exhausted. This whole journey has been intense. Yes, I want to meet all those people out there and learn how I can serve them as the sovereign of the castle. Yes, I'd love a gorgeous wardrobe. And yes, I want to know more about my Secret Garden. But I am simply exhausted.

Laura must have felt my exhaustion, because she looks at me with the kindest eyes.

"It feels like you have a bit of an internal log jam — just like the one you can see over there, damming up the stream a bit — where the flow of all your new experiences and inner knowing have met up with some debris of your old patterns and beliefs. It's as if everything is trying to squeeze through too small an opening at once. Why don't you lie down here," she says, pointing to a soft patch of grass next to the little stream, "and close your eyes for a few minutes?"

She continues: "Imagine the water rushing through you, beginning to loosen up that old unnecessary debris, and eventually taking it all with it. There's nothing for you to do but to relax and imagine yourself becoming really spacious and letting the strength of the water's flow do its work."

I follow Laura's invitation to rest. The degree of my exhaustion becomes obvious when I lie down and my whole body just puddles onto the grass.

The next thing I know is that I am slowly waking up from a deep, deep sleep. *Where am I?* And then I remember: I am in my Secret Garden. I see Laura crouching a few feet away by the water, tearing off bits of grass and letting them float away, carried by clear water. The little dam she pointed out before is gone. She is wearing her pink jacket again. How did she get it? I never knew that I took it off.

"How are you feeling?" she asks, when she becomes aware that I am stirring.

I take a few deep breaths and notice that I feel much more clear now. Strong again, yet very soft and receptive at the same time.

"Look at this stream." Laura beckons me to sit next to her. "See how the water is clear and very adaptable — how it flows softly around and over all the rocks? Yet we all know about the enormous strength water has. And look how easily it carries along little bits of debris, like the pieces of grass I'm throwing in, now that the logjam is cleared. Whenever you can stay present, lean in, feel what there is to feel, stay in your truth, and don't suppress or ignore the issues and challenges that arise in your life, your beautiful inner flow has the capacity to clear all those bits and pieces — even the slightly bigger ones — with ease, and remain uninterrupted in its happy, flowing, gurgling journey."

"Nice jacket, by the way," I wink at Laura. She laughs.

"Yes, I took it back because it's important for you to feel and know your own truth very clearly right now, not truth that's filtered or obstructed by anybody else's input — not even by my love."

Coming home — home to myself
Rooted in the ever-expanding solidity of my own universe
My breath, my connection to life in all dimensions
Breathing in all aspects of me
Breathing out my love for you

# 16

FREEDOM!!! Space to be me. Space to *feel* me. Space to explore my Secret Garden.

*Ahhh* :) I deeply inhale the warm fragrant air, closing my eyes for a moment to follow its trail down into the depth of my body more closely. I feel incredibly awake, incredibly light, and incredibly alive, now that the logjam has been cleared and the drowsiness of my nap has vanished. I know how my eyes must be flashing beams of light when I turn to Laura.

"Would it be ok if I explore my Secret Garden by myself for a little while?"

"Of course! This is *your* special place. I will be right here watching your flow," she beams back.

I can't help the big, huge smile that appears on my face. I am so excited about what I might find as I set out towards the bright flowers. But just as I reach the first ones, my attention gets drawn to a tiny trapdoor in the lawn to my right. It is dwarf- or fairy-sized, and as I look it begins shrinking, until it has basically vanished. This makes me think of "Alice in Wonderland's" rabbit hole.

*"What does that have to do with me?"* I wonder. I don't like weirdly twisted stuff. I like clarity, spaciousness, beauty . . . depth — yes, but a spacious, clear kind of depth. As I clarify this for myself, the last minuscule remainder of the trapdoor vanishes — actually, pops, like the tiniest of bubbles. This makes me giggle involuntary.

I move forward, deeper into the millions of flowers. Here and there, I see another one of those small trap doors; they all shrink and pop whenever I look at them. It must be contagious for the other trap doors, still hidden from my view — because, abruptly, I feel as if I'm in a flower-filled champagne glass. The flower garden flooded with the effervescence of thousands of little bubbles popping all over. I have a serious case of the giggles, now. I throw up my arms, tilt back my head, and, laughing, openly start spinning in a circle.

Such joy, such freedom! Still laughing and a little out of breath, I stop spinning and sit down on a little clearing amidst the flowers. Then I notice a bee flying up to me. Why does she feel like a greeting committee? Hmmm….

"Hello, Dear One, we are so happy to see you here," the bee addresses me. "I would like to show you something that goes beyond your previous ability to perceive things. I would like to show you the Rainbow Dimension."

I *love* the sound of that: Rainbow Dimension :)! It sounds bright, beautiful, colorful — like a place where everything is possible, but in an open, spacious, and clear way. "Somewhere over the rainbow…." I have to laugh that I don't find it odd at all that I am talking to a bee. Why *wouldn't* I talk to a bee? I chuckle to myself. It doesn't seem like my new bee friend has a name, though — just a number, which appears to be *153*.

*153 — a number, not a name. Hmmm…. I looked up the meaning, and this is what I found: "Angel number 153 carries a message that you are being called to use your creativity and leadership skills in the service of all humanity. Whenever the highly auspicious energy of angel number 153 shows up in your experience, it is a sign to look for ways that you can use your talents and opportunities to serve others." (https:// thesecretofthetarot.com/angel-number-153/)*

*I also remember a story that a beekeeper-friend told me, that he believed bees to be fifth-dimensional beings. The same friend also told me a story about when he and three friends were hiking in Sedona a few years ago, and observed a rainbow snake. It seemed as if they had entered a space where everything looked completely different, and way more*

Claudia Sasse

*vivid around them. At the same time, they could not be seen by other hikers on the path anymore.*

"So how do we get there, 153?" I ask, curious and a little excited.

Can bees smile? It feels like she smiles when she says, "You get there in a way that has become quite familiar to you recently: through the openness and spaciousness of your heart. This time, you add something else, though — your ability to see-feel with your third eye. Your capacity to imagine your own desires *and* receive information from Source, *while* staying firmly anchored in your heart, will open this whole new dimension for you."

I know this should sound complicated to me, but it doesn't. It feels light, joyful, spacious, and incredibly easy, somehow. I flash 153 a big bright smile, take a deep breath into my heart, and allow the swirling color palette of the flowers and the soft buzzing of 153's flight pattern around me to take me into the imagination of my third eye. I usually need to close my eyes whenever I try to see with my third eye, but in this case I leave them open, curious about what else I might be able to perceive. I feel incredibly turned on, as if I am pure creative force. Bright and stunningly colorful pictures begin flashing in front of my eyes. "Colorful" does not even begin to describe it, though. The colors look unlike any I have ever seen before. And I not only can I see them, but I receive them with *all* my senses. I can taste, feel, hear, and *know* them.

153's talking about imagining my desires makes me think of the retreat, again. I can see it: the lush, rich, fertile powerful land, the farm, the retreat buildings, the people deeply in touch with their own truth, doing what brings them the most joy, connecting with each other in a powerfully open-hearted way where all energy systems fully merge in and out of each other. And now the flowers of my Secret Garden are merging with that vision.

And then, yet another layer comes in. I can see different kinds of buildings — white, luminous, many having sides made out of crystals. There are temple-like structures and people — as luminous as the buildings — dressed in a variety of flowing styles of white shimmering light. I become faintly aware of even more layers, but I don't go into them, so as not to overwhelm myself.

I am sitting there in awe — being, perceiving, breathing it all in — when I feel myself being catapulted right smack into the middle of my vision.

Heavens align
To create the magic
That once was only visible to our mind's eye
As we stand there in awe at
How this all came to be

# 17

Seriously? This is amazing! I feel lightheaded, exhilarated, and giddy — like I just came out of my favorite carnival ride. And at the same time, my heart is so full it's almost ready to burst.

And then it does. It bursts open. Which makes me laugh even more with this overflowing joy and a gratitude that is so deeply anchored, it goes on forever.

I am clearly not alone in this space. The people I had envisioned before are here. When I look closely, I recognize them from the castle garden. I guess those are "my people" — and no matter where my world is, I am connected to them and they will be in it. Now I *really, really* want to meet them. Talk to them, get to know what their lives are like, their experiences, their dreams.

Looking down, I notice that I am wearing something different — a glowing white dress. It reminds me of the shimmering light-clothes of the luminous people I saw earlier in my vision. My dress feels light as air and, yes, light as light. It flows around me like an extended expression of myself. This has nothing to do with clothing as I've known it until now. I feel buoyant, beautiful, and free.

I guess after all this time of receiving, learning, and being propelled and guided into new worlds, it is time to make a move of some sort. I feel ready and excited.

I see that I have "landed" in the middle of two paths crossing. I have the choice of going either uphill, downhill, left, or right. Hmmm . . . which direction feels the most open, promising, light, juicy? Where do I feel most invited to go? I close my eyes for a second, take a deep sweet breath, and feel a big smile spread across my face. I am being guided to the right — in the direction of the magical valley.

I have only walked a few steps when I see two women and a man sitting at a wooden picnic table, playing a game with dice of many colors — blue, red, yellow, green, purple, orange…. all the chakra colors are present. And then there are some dice with ever-changing colors that have more to do with the intense shimmering luminosity of the colors in the Rainbow Dimension. The picnic table is framed by dense dark-green bushes that block the open, spacious view of the ocean, otherwise easily visible from most of the land. It's a bit colder and darker here, overall, than where I came from just up the path.

"Hi," I lift my hand in a greeting as I approach the table. "This looks really interesting. Would you mind if I join you?"

The people in this group do not seem to have been part of the castle-garden group, and all have their eyes glued to the dice. Finally, one of the women looks up with a curious mixture of hope, desperation, and profound wisdom in her face.

"This is a very complicated game," she explains to me, "one that you cannot simply join. It has taken *lifetimes* of studying and practice to be at our level." Her voice has the exasperated patience of a college professor denying a first grader access to her class.

"Oh yes, of course, please excuse the interruption," I reply, as I bow out of the dark, enclosed space around the picnic table. I feel slightly annoyed, and definitely not as buoyant anymore. Why was I guided *here*, of all places?

"To experience *very* clearly who are *not* your people," I hear in a buzzy kind of way. And then I see her. 153 is in da house! "Now that you have this contrast," 153 continues, "it will make it even more obvious when you encounter those with whom you have a heart connection — those whom you are meant to serve, and those who are meant to serve you.

Those who you are meant to love, and those who are meant to love you."

Scarcely have I noticed her when she takes off, flying ahead of me at breakneck/break-wing speed. I have to run to keep up with her. All the while, she is not flying in a straight line, but changing directions, flying around curves, and generally doing her bee dance, while I run after her, laughing.

"Stop!" I cry, eventually coming to a halt somewhere in a wide-open field, still laughing and totally out of breath. "OMG, 153, what was *that* about?" I ask, breathing rapidly. As I bend over and grab my knees for support, I can feel-see-hear how she giggles.

"That was literally the fastest way to snap you back into the joy and lightness of your own body, wisdom, and energy field. Your endorphins are pumping again. So is your heart. Out of habit, you could have easily overanalyzed your recent encounter, tried to learn their game, and made yourself fit into their experience. Except, that would have completely dimmed your beautiful luminous energy, *and* it would not have helped them, either. You are simply not each other's people."

"So where are *my* people, then?" I inquire. "I thought I saw some of them before, but now all I can see is this open field and beautiful nature all around us."

"How about you sit down for a minute and catch your breath some more. You just learned from those other people how important the game that they are playing is for them." And then 153 invites me, "Why don't you tell me from your heart what is important to *you*?"

I sit down on the soft, bouncy grass and tilt my head back to feel the sun on my face. "The sun...," I tell her. "LIGHT, CLARITY and JOY are important to me. And the SPACIOUSNESS and OPENNESS of this field, from where I can look far out over the ocean and towards the lush abundance of the valley. Actually, ABUNDANCE is also important to me — the juiciness, richness, and freedom of this land and of true abundance. And, yes,

FREEDOM, the EASE and spaciousness of being your true, whole, independent, sovereign self. TRUTH, WHOLENESS, and SOVEREIGNTY, as well. And the ADVENTURE of EXPANSION and discovering new possibilities, as well as the SWEETNESS and BEAUTY of DEEP HEART CONNECTIONS."

And as I think about all those beautiful heart connections I had felt in the castle garden, something else bubbles up with the effervescence of champagne, and I add: "SERVICE! I want to serve. I want to share all those beautiful things I have learned and will continue to learn. I want to share the ease, lightness, happiness, and freedom that seem possible for all of us. I want to share the love."

*This reminds me of a question a mentor of mine recently asked: "What do you stand for?" And my answer was: "I stand for truth — the truth that lives in our hearts. I stand for spaciousness, freedom, joy, ease, and lightness. I stand for inclusivity and tearing walls down instead of building them up. I stand for mutual respect and peace. I stand for recognizing each other's brilliance and coming together as people, not as roles and titles. I stand for expansion and continuously opening to new possibilities. I stand for the sovereignty and wholeness of each and every one of us. I stand for love in all its forms. And I know that heaven on earth IS possible."*

Mmmmh, yes, that feels good. So does the sun on my face. I had not really looked at 153 while I was talking, and now I notice something changing next to me: the bee is morphing into a human figure that looks like King Henry VIII, just stepped straight out of his renaissance castle onto our lush tropical field. His heavy, bejeweled brocade, velvet, and ermine clothing looks decidedly out of place. And why is my bee friend a man, all of a sudden?

"No worries, I am only projecting this image to help you experience something," I hear 153.

King Henry VIII seems to be just about the *opposite* of what I have just declared as important to me — selfish, ruthless, charismatic, but a bit pompous- and stuffy-looking in all his bejeweled splendor. To me ease, lightness, and freedom definitely looks different from him. Instead of connecting to hearts, he severs heads. And although I have no way of knowing, it also feels like he uses his charisma in a mean, manipulative kind of way, so instead of serving his people he uses them. His presence makes me feel uneasy in a throat-constricting kind of way. I feel almost strangled, as if the access to the airflow of my enthusiasm and lightness from just a minute ago is completely cut off.

"You have been learning about your *bright* side as a sovereign," I hear 153 explain. "This is the shadow side."

Whoa, this is intense! "This is my shadow side??? OMG, 153, I cannot possibly meet any of my people now. How would I know which version of me would come out? I don't want to subject anyone to *this* guy! I might cut off heads." I jump up and pace in front of Henry VIII's projection like a tiger in a cage. I want to run away as far as I can, but I know I can't escape him if he is my shadow. Shit! I feel completely trapped — trapped by my own shadow, of all things. "What can I *do*, 153?" I cry. I must look completely haunted and desperate, and my frantic pace gets me nowhere.

"Stop for a second and look at Henry," 153 transmits calmly. "Look him in the eyes. What do you see?"

"I see a man who looks haunted — and sad, somehow, as if clouds of betrayal and hurt are obstructing his clear vision. I see the courage and resolve to go on anyway and fulfill his role as king. I can see a longing to be loved as a man, not as a king. I can see the sweetness and softness of a 13-year-old writing poetry, looking at the world in wonder, yet wanting to explore its edges and needing to be brave at the same time. I can see a thoughtful young man being hyped up and pushed out in front of the masses as their new strong ruler. Wow, this looks like a person I would actually like to meet! Something must have happened to turn him into the ruthless Henry VIII we have all learned about."

"Yes, many difficult and often terrible things happened. He is a product of his time, his role, his circumstances, and his character predisposition," 153 agrees.

And now, instead of wanting to escape, I feel more curiosity and compassion for this shadow side of myself. Although it does not seem *quite* like myself. Obviously, in this life I have not had the same experiences as a renaissance king.

"Yes, that's right. It's not the same. Henry is a projection of what is going on inside of you. A real person, yet not you — so you can look at him with compassion, once you see what's behind his rough shadow-behavior. So why don't you keep looking at him through the eyes of love and compassion?" 153 invites me.

As I do that, I also remember the light codes. *"Can we activate those here?"* I wonder.

"Yes, we can," 153's transmission comes through with a smile.

I can feel my heart opening as the light codes begin flooding the scene. And then I can actually see behind all stories, and all I see is Henry's wholeness and perfection. Eventually his projection actually speaks: "Thank you for seeing me," he says with a lovely British accent, as his figure dissolves in a ball of sunlight.

Claudia Sasse

When loving you is the freedom to be me

# 18

*For a moment in time, life has taken over and I have seemingly removed myself from the story — from writing this book. Yet as I tap into its energy again and open my heart to the heart of the story, I have the odd sensation that the essence of the story, everything I have experienced since finishing the last chapter, and everything I want to bring into being in my life, is coming together in a spiral dance of creation.*

After Henry is gone, I sit on the grass, turn my face up towards the sun, and simply breathe in the sweet air for a moment. A gentle breeze caresses me, softly playing with my skin, my hair. I feel alive, part of my environment, absorbed in its energy. It feels as if Henry took a barrier with him when he vanished, one that hadn't allowed me to fully know how I was truly a fragment of all of it, yet at the same time whole and complete within myself.

*All here now!* shoots through my head. It's all here now, *I* am all here now — not fragmented by rejecting a part of myself. It feels like all parts of me have spiraled together — and while I am pretty much in the same position as when Henry appeared, everything feels different, like I am peacefully resting within myself. So what is possible with *all* of me here?

I look over to 153 and see that she has morphed yet again — this time, into a young princess, maybe 18 years old. She is dressed in a white long gown made out of shimmery heavy silk that is slightly too big and slightly smudged. Judging from the type of dress, it also looks like she should be wearing a corset, but she is not. Most of her long hair is swept up in an artfully intricate hairdo, but many wavy blonde strands have escaped from their proper place and are dancing in the wind.

Bits and pieces of nature seem to have found a new home in her hair, and these add to her slightly disheveled but somehow free appearance. She is laughing, with her head thrown back and her eyes cast upward, and twirling on the grass in an exuberant, wildly free the-hills-are-alive-Julie-Andrews kind of way. And when she finally plops down on the grass next to me, slightly out of breath and beaming flashes of light, she reminds me of Laura.

"Hi, I am SweetPea," she smiles.

"SweetPea?" I have to laugh. "Really, that's your name??"

"Well, that's what everyone calls me," she chuckles. "My actual name is like *really* long and *really* complicated — and *really* boring."

"Ok, SweetPea it is, then," I grin. "It's a pleasure to make your acquaintance, your Highness. It seems to me that you *are* a princess of some sort, right?" I ask.

"OMG, YES!! Totally!" she beams. "I LOVE talking like a California valley girl when I am out here, by the way. Because in the palace, I always have to speak properly. Proper anything is SO incredibly boring."

"Well, you can talk any which way you like with me, SweetPea," I smile. "I'm a little bit curious, though, who you are — and why we would meet here in the middle of this hill, in a place that looks and feels like the land of the retreat space that I have been dreaming about. How did *you* get here?"

"Oh, I'm like totally a part of you," she says matter-of-factly. "That's why I am here. Looks like it was time for us to meet in person."

"A part of me . . . like Henry, my shadow?" I inquire.

"Yes, totally like Henry," she giggles, "just waaay cuter."

"So one part of me is a free-spirited, slightly rebellious, exuberant princess?"

"Yep, you like totally got it! Come on, let's go!! I want to show you something."

Claudia Sasse

She jumps up, brimming with boundless energy and excitement. Once I have gotten up as well, she takes my hand and we run across the hill to the left, away from the valley, back towards town. Actually, it feels more like we are *flying* across the hill, despite the fact that our feet are lightly touching the ground. When we reach a strip of Koa trees, she slows down and begins weaving through the little forest while looking up at the trees with a mixture of awe, adoration, and love. I can't help but feeling that SweetPea is introducing me to some very old, very wise friends.

"Listen!" she whispers. "Can you feel it? Can you hear it? They are calling you, inviting you, talking to you."

The crowns of the trees are swaying like ocean waves above our heads. The little forest feels peaceful, sheltered, safe, yet open and free — full of new life, and yet ancient at the same time. I find myself taking deep breaths, immersing myself in the calm aliveness of the space. And I know that I am smiling — peacefully smiling.

I let go of SweetPea's hand and walk up to one of the trees, resting first my left hand, then, after a few moments, both hands on its smooth trunk. But instead of hearing or feeling what the tree has to say, I am being shown a picture, a scene of some sort. The view oscillates between a wide bay with yellow sand, framed by cliffs dotted with Koa trees, and a golden field of harvested grain that could be somewhere in northern Europe, framed by a leafy-tree forest. Both scenes are drenched in the rich, sweet, and gentle golden light of the glowing evening sun. I can feel how both pieces of land are connected somehow, apparently partially because of the trees' communication with one another.

*I have to think about how we are cutting down more and more beautiful trees on our planet — and a picture of bulldozers in front of a forest briefly shoots through my head.*

"This is not what we want to show you," I hear the whisper of a calm and gentle, incredibly sweet female voice, "as this is not for you to take care of. It is your job to reintroduce people to their profound connection to nature, to the healing power of the land, the trees, the waters, the rocks — to the deep communion that is possible between all beings on this planet. You are not even the one to tell them what they might be able to perceive. It is only your task to *invite* them, open up the *possibilities*, and give them the space to have their own experiences of connection — which, in many cases, actually will be much deeper than your own experience. Breathe with me! Feel how we are inhaling and exhaling in the perfect symbiotic dance of the breath of life."

I move closer to the tree, allowing my whole body to rest against its trunk as I breathe in and out, feeling my breaths become calmer and deeper. It almost feels as if I am entering the tree.

"You can feel yourself becoming one with me, can't you?" I hear the tree's sweet voice.

"Yes," I say softly, as I feel myself melting into the Koa tree, feeling the rhythm of our breath flowing together in a gentle circle of life. Yet at the same time, I am aware of the circular pattern of my own inhale and exhale as well as the tree's serene independent breathing: both of our self-contained systems the opposite of each other, yet vital for sustaining each other.

After a while of this deep blissful connection with the Koa tree, I feel it is time to move on, and I thank the tree from the bottom of my heart for sharing herself with me. As my eyes begin searching for SweetPea, I see her hugging another tree close by. Her cheek is pressed against its trunk and she has an angelic smile on her face. I don't want to interrupt her rapture, but she must have sensed my attention and peels herself off the tree after a moment.

Claudia Sasse

She is not quite willing to let go; one hand still lingers on the tree's trunk as she says, "Isn't this incredible?" with the most tender voice.

"Yes, I am still in awe," I more breathe than say, not quite wanting to break the magic all around us with any loud sound, "and I can feel the breath of the trees all around us. Thank you so much for showing me this place."

"You have always known this place," SweetPea smiles softly. "I am just the part of you that is reminding you of it."

KOA
Sacred tree
Ancient connection to all of life
Healer — Master — Keeper of Wisdom
Root and crown
Anchor and wave
Sweetness and strength
Living in sacred community
Yet standing along

# 19

"Where do we go from here?" I ask SweetPea, with a deep exhale that feels like I am leaving the trees a gift as we get ready to head . . . where, I don't know yet. All I know is that I feel incredibly open and spacious. I notice a ravine beyond the little Koa forest. A misty layer of clouds has rolled into the little valley, shrouding its tall trees and tangled jungle vines in an air of mystery that is somehow vying for my attention. "Is that where we'll go next?" I ask the princess, pointing towards the direction of the ravine.

For a moment, SweetPea's face loses its playfulness. She looks straight at me with the clearest, deepest eyes and says, "It's actually your choice. Check in with yourself for a second. Where do you want to take this sweet open spaciousness you are feeling right now — down into your fascination with the mystery of the wet jungle, or back out into the wide-open sunny grass area?"

Wow! My head immediately whips to the right, in the direction of the open expanse of the field. The thought of being out in the bright sunshine makes me breathe deeply and puts a big smile on my face, whereas the thought of going down into the ravine makes me feel uneasy and constricted, as if the tangly vines are growing all over me instead of the trees. The open field, however, feels filled with promise and possibilities, and suddenly I can't wait to get back there.

"Trust your inner guidance system," SweetPea says. "It knows, even if your head doesn't."

This time, it is I who take the lead. "Come on, SweetPea!" I say, taking her hand. "It feels like we need to go back to the field. I don't know *why*, exactly, but somehow I am really excited about it." I can almost feel the trees at my back smiling and ushering us out, like sweet mommies sending their kids out into the adventures of their lives. Before we leave, though, I let go of SweetPea's hand for a moment, turn around, put my hands together, and place them first on my forehead and then my on my heart, silently saying "thank you" for the gift of the trees' presence. Next to me, SweetPea is doing the same.

"Ok, girlfriend, let's go!!" I call, pulling her along. It feels as if we are flying out of the trees and across the field, until we come to a point where the open field meets a happily gurgling stream framed by light leafy trees that look a little like birch trees. I feel like I want to follow the flow of the water. While there are plenty of beautiful boulders in the little river to hop over, we find an easy, mostly shallow path on its side. After a little while, something feels and sounds different, though, and causes me to proceed with a bit more caution.

And then I see why: The gentle slope abruptly ends at a steep cliff, and the tame stream turns into a tumbling waterfall. Because I have sensed that something was changing, we have slowed down enough that I don't get spooked by this sudden change of scenery — almost to the contrary. I am a little nervous looking down into the depth in front of us, but I am mostly excited, inspired, grateful for this beautiful discovery. The rushing water falls into an emerald-green-and-blue pool that sparkles with sunlight, looks almost otherworldly, and makes me feel *very* alive. "Look at this, SweetPea!" I exclaim. "What an absolutely magnificent surprise. And look at that pool: it looks like a liquid gemstone. I wonder how we can get down there?" I say, eyeing the steep cliffs on both sides. "I guess we could backtrack and go waaaay around."

"Looks like we need to use the Rainbow Bridge," SweetPea suggests matter-of-factly.

"The Rainbow Bridge?? Um, what exactly is that?" I ask, a bit confused.

"It's like totally the fun and easy way to move in, out, and inside the Rainbow dimension," SweetPea explains.

Claudia Sasse

"Remember when you felt like you were catapulted here after opening and anchoring yourself in your heart, imagining this place with all of your inner third-eye senses and opening to receiving the guidance of Source? You traveled over the Rainbow Bridge. So imagine yourself being down there by the pool. Feel it, breathe it, KNOW it."

Hmmm, does this have something to do with teleporting? I am quite curious, since moving swiftly from one location to the next has definitely been on my list of things I want to be able to do.

I open my heart even more to the deep, jewel-toned pool, and see myself sitting on a rock by its side until I know with every fiber of my being what it is like to be there. I can smell the slight coolness of its blue-green depth, feel the occasional spray of the waterfall on my face, see the play of the sunlight even more brilliantly. Except . . . I am still at the top of the waterfall. "Hmmm, SweetPea, I don't know, are you sure about this?" I say, a little disappointed. "I just did the whole imagining thing and I am still here. What else do I need to do?"

"Actually, it's like totally *not* about doing," SweetPea answers, letting her valley-girl-self loose again. "It's about letting go, surrendering, and opening to receiving."

"Oh geez, SweetPea, and how am I supposed to do *that*?"

"Well, you know that breathing thing, don't ya?"

"Yeeees . . . and?"

"Our breath," she explains, "while seemingly the most basic and simple thing that keeps us alive, has an incredible number of layers and dimensions, and is — among other things — actually a multi-faceted technological tool. In this case, imagine receiving the place you *want* to be — the pool at the bottom of the waterfall — with every in-breath, while you let go of the place you are *currently* at with every out-breath."

"Ok, so that's the receiving and letting-go part. But what about the surrender? Will I have to let go of wanting to even go down there?" I inquire, a bit unnerved. This is beginning to feel *way* too complicated, like it has nothing to do with the lightness of the Rainbow Dimension anymore."

For some reason, that causes pearls of laughter to come from SweetPea. In fact, she laughs so hard that she is holding her belly and gasping for air after a while. "NEVER let go of your heart's desires — maybe the specificity, but definitely not of the feeling of them," she gasps after a while, eyes sparkling, and wiping tears of laughter from her face. "Just let go of your insistence to micromanage their delivery. You will receive everything with the perfection of divine timing, and sometimes it will look different than you thought."

"What is so funny about this?" I ask a bit indignantly."

"Oh, I just had a vision of what would happen if you used the breathing technology I just told you about, and forced your way through the Rainbow Dimension without the surrender part. You'd keep face-planting in the cutest way. You'd never really get hurt, but it looks funny . . . and you always have a really confused look on your face." She begins laughing yet again. And I can't help but laugh with her.

"So how do I *not* keep face-planting, then?" I chuckle.

"Know that you are part of a bigger system, and that there really *is* divine timing for everything. Trust for things to unfold for your highest good *and* the highest good for all. FEEL yourself being grateful for that. And then, simply play and have fun. Breathe *in* the pool . . . breathe *out* right here, the place at the top of the waterfall. And next thing you know, you might find yourself down by the pool — or not, if something even better is waiting for you elsewhere."

Somehow a pressure that I didn't even know I'd felt about figuring out this teleporting thing has been lifted. The effervescence of SweetPea's laughter-pearls are still lingering in the air like a tapestry of light, bubbling around and out of me as I breathe in the beautiful pool of water down at the bottom of the waterfall, feeling its coolness and the water spraying down from the falls, and as I exhale our place at the top. After a short, while the air around me takes on another quality, as if it just became more dense. I ask SweetPea if it is still a good idea to keep up my breathing exercise, and I hear-feel an emphatic "*absolutely.*" So I sit there, breathe, and smile while the air around me begins to feel even more substantial. And then in a flash, something shifts — and when I blink, I am looking at the waterfall right in front of me. I hear SweetPea going "WHEE!!" as she lands next to me at the side of the pool. Somehow, I could swear that I literally just saw her sliding down a rainbow bridge.

When I share this with her, she replies, "Yes, I totally did. As I am a projection, I get to do what *you* wish you could. Who knows, maybe you'll get to play like this soon, too," she says with a wink.

# THE WELL WITHIN

The waters of life shifting, changing
Yet remaining the same
Easily moving between dimensions
Embracing
Carrying many
Or focusing on one

Be at peace with the flow of life
As all is fed from the deep well within

# 20

I am sitting on a rock facing the waterfall. The tall trees that grow in a half-circle around the deep, clear, green-blue pool provide shelter around my back. The cliffs framing the waterfall are covered with velvety dark-green moss accented, with fountains of bright green fern. The top, where I just came from, is glowing in the sun. Where I am sitting, the sunshine is dancing on the water, while the cliff is in the shadows, giving the scene an air of mystery. I am briefly curious why I would have chosen to enter this mysterious place instead of staying in the bright sunshine and the spaciousness at the top. Except that — unlike the foggy gulch I decided not to enter — this place feels sacred. I also have a sense that SweetPea has quietly retreated and left this place for me to experience on my own.

The pool — a mixture of mystery and clarity on its outer edges — is penetrated by the rushing curtain of the waterfall, which adds a light, frothy layer of inevitability and determination to the scene. I sit still, closing my eyes, feeling the spray of the water cooling my face. And when I open them again, I see a row of people standing in the shadow against the cliff on either side of the waterfall, with a few more people appearing from behind it. They look familiar and unfamiliar at the same time — as if I know them, but not their specific appearance.

A man whose hair is wrapped in a piece of cloth in what looks like a ceremonial way steps forward (walking on the water!!!), until he comes to a halt in front of me. He holds his hands out, revealing what looks to be a richly decorated ceremonial pipe.

"Please take this sacred pipe as an offering from all of us," he says in a deeply resonant voice that echoes all around me.

"Who are you?" I ask him. "You look like I should know you all, but I don't, not really."

"We are representations of the different people in your life — your friends, your family, your kids, your lovers, your clients. We are the ones who trigger any of the remaining shadow pieces within you," the man explains.

Is he a monk, a medicine man, or a priest of some sort?

*He reminds me a little of KenLa, a very sweet, wise, and spiritually connected man I met at a few seminars many years ago.*

"The time has come to let those shadow pieces go so we can all meet in the light," he addresses me. "In a moment, I will invite you to receive this pipe. It is the Pipe of Truth. Take a deep breath, blow into it, and then set it down to your left. Then I will ask you to enter the pool and swim through it to the backside of the waterfall. The temperature of the pool will vary anywhere from pleasantly warm to freezing cold, depending on what will be the most supportive for you during this special task. It will be most beneficial and easiest if you don't question this but simply trust that you are cared for and assisted. I will wait for you behind the waterfall. Before you begin, we will invite the gods, goddesses, ascended masters, angels, and light beings that will be most able to assist you during this procedure. Are you willing to accept this task?" he asks, looking at me with the kindest yet most determined eyes that leave no real space for escaping what is to unfold next.

"Yes," I nod, slightly apprehensive but silently relieved at the same time. "Yes, I am willing to accept this task," I say with more conviction, now.

The Wise Man waves the pipe in a circle, and the most beautiful luminous beings appear in multiple circles all around

Claudia Sasse

us. Some are standing on the ground around the pool; others are in stages of elevation, as if they are standing on the steps of an invisible amphitheater. Somehow I had expected the scene to remain serene and hushed. However, what is unfolding around me looks and feels more like a party. I hear laughter, and excited, mostly telepathic, conversations. I see hugs, fist pumps, beings waving to each other across the pool. I see some dance moves to inaudible music and a couple of little kids surfing invisible waves in the air.

The Wise Man smiles, waves at the crowd, and looks back at me. "Aren't they beautiful? I always love it when I get to see them." Then he puts all his focus back on me and asks me, "Are you ready?"

"Yes, I am ready," I reply, eager to begin.

The Wise Man takes the pipe, inhales, and blows air into its mouthpiece. Three white irregular rings like clouds without a center appear above the pipe. Interesting … doesn't one usually suck the smoke *in* when smoking a pipe? He hands the pipe to me, motioning to do the same as he has done. As I take the pipe, the crowd goes silent and I can feel their love surrounding me.

I inhale deeply, bring the mouthpiece up to my mouth, briefly close my eyes, and then exhale into the pipe. I also see three cloud rings appear above it. However, only one is white: the others are yellow and red. I have a sense that there might be a black one as well, but it is not visible, as if it remains under the surface. I don't really know what it all means, and somehow I don't actually care. It's as if I have entered a space where my only focus is the next step I need to take.

The Wise Man has disappeared. I place the pipe on my left side as I was told, get up from the rock I am sitting on, step towards the pool, and begin walking into the water, still wearing my luminous dress. The water is COLD, freezing cold — but I keep going, my eyes glued to the waterfall in front of me. It's almost as if I fell into a trance when I blew into the pipe. When I am immersed in the water up to my bellybutton, I begin swimming. The ice-cold water makes my heart flutter, and I gasp for air. I try to relax — trusting. Trusting that I am indeed supported. Trusting that I *will* be ok, that I *am* ok in this moment. Trusting that whatever I am doing here *is* indeed for my wellbeing and my highest good.

When I arrive at the waterfall, my heart is skipping beats and I am breathing erratically. I *need* to get to the other side. *now!* Not quite sure what to do I take as deep a breath as I can, under the circumstances, hold it, and keep on swimming.

I am surprised that when I swim into the waterfall, it actually feels soft and sweet, like a gentle liquid curtain. Once I have crossed its threshold, I am in a completely different world. The water temperature feels perfect and balmy. I find myself in something like a bright cave basking in white, yellow, and red light — the colors of the cloud rings. My erratic heartbeat begins to calm down, and when I try to stand up my feet find a hold on solid rock. The Wise Man is here, sitting against the back wall on a large rock that reminds me of a throne. The shadow people, as I silently call them, have joined him and are lined up on both sides of the throne.

The Wise Man smiles warmly. "Congratulations — you prevailed. This was a hard test for your heart and your ability to trust. Know that this test has not been offered to you by an outside source, but that you have chosen to give it to yourself. All of us are only here to help you facilitate your expansion."

I am standing there on the rock, two-thirds of my body still immersed in the water, blinking away the water droplets, when — without any warning — tears begin falling out of my eyes. A wealth of emotions, long-buried and forgotten, are making their way to the surface, rolling in like waves, each one slightly different, yet in a steady rhythm.

Trying to stop this would be like trying to stop the waves in the ocean. All I can do is stand there and feel, and cry, and let all these emotions wash over and through me. The yellow, red, and white lights come alive and wash over and through me, as well. The lights seem to have something to do with the chakra colors, I notice. The yellow light makes me feel more empowered, while the red light gives me a feeling of home. The white light, however, feels very clear and expansive. As I am feeling and crying and bathing in the light, and my tears are mingling with the water of the pool, the shadow people begin disappearing — more like dissolving — one by one, until only the Wise Man is left sitting in front of me.

He gets up from the rock throne, and beckons for me to come out of the water and sit down in his place. Unexpectedly, I feel light as a feather, happy, giddy, even — filled with endless energy. I jump out of the pool and take a seat on the throne. The color of the light around me has changed. It looks brighter, clear. The curtain of the waterfall shimmers like rainbow diamonds falling from the sky. And the little cave feels huge, suddenly — incredibly spacious and expansive.

The Wise Man steps out onto the water and produces the Pipe of Truth again. In some way, he must have gotten it from where I had left it. He smiles, and the large, clear teardrop crystal attached to his headdress right on top of his third eye begins glowing in rainbow colors.

"You have dared to enter the pool and face the truth of your buried emotions without resistance, and you have transformed," he addresses me lovingly. "Take a breath and blow into the Pipe of Truth again."

I bow my head in recognition and gratitude as I receive the pipe from his finely sculpted hands. For a moment I simply feel the beautiful rich energy of the pipe in my own hands. How many have received this pipe before me and gone through this process? How many have gone through the process of feeling the truth of their long-buried emotions? I feel such gratitude for each and every one of them. It seems like they have paved the way for me, for the freedom and lightness I am feeling right now.

Eventually I close my eyes, inhale deeply, and blow into the pipe. Three rings emerge, all showing all the colors of the rainbow. "Welcome to the Rainbow Realms, Dear One," the Wise Man says warmly, as he takes the pipe from me with a slight bow. His eyes have changed, and I can see rainbow colors sparkling in them. *Do my eyes shine in rainbow colors now too?* I wonder. "Yes, they do," he smiles. "I am KenLa, by the way. I am a version of your friend in real life."

*That surprises me. The only name that is coming forward is KenLa's real name. I will have to ask KenLa for his consent to use it, obviously.... Hmmm....*

I sit on my throne smiling, and allow the clear, sparkly rainbow light to caress me. It feels like my whole body is absorbing it, resonating, even communicating with it. It's a completely new sensation, beyond thought. I almost feel like I am dissolving into this light while still being aware of my individual, yet much more pliable, form. I am moving, dancing, shifting into ever-new form with this light — a little like these colorful, slightly psychedelic screensaver programs. Except this is much, much lighter and incredibly clear.

"What now?" I ask KenLa after a while. I have no idea how long I have been sitting there. Time, as I know it, does not seem to exist here. I feel peaceful, clear, and also a little turned on — excited.

"Are you ready to go back out into the rest of the world?" KenLa replies. He is sitting cross-legged, slightly to my right, on the water facing the waterfall by now.

"Yes, I am!" I say, feeling ready and excited to meet life in all colors of the rainbow.

"So where do you want to go?" KenLa asks evenly.

Claudia Sasse

# LOVE

There is always more. . . .
more love to feel
to expand into
to be
to radiate
to allow
to receive
to give
And yet. . . .
Love simply is ALL

# 21

"I want to go out into the real world," I hear myself reply.

"What does that mean to you?" he questions evenly, his kind face displaying no emotions.

"I have learned and experienced so much on this journey so far: presence, my own universe, the light codes, the Well of Oneness and the massive receiving from the Moon Maiden, forgiveness, the power of the Merkabah, speaking from my heart, being the sovereign of my own castle, and my connection to all. I've trusted, seen one of my biggest dreams, loved my shadow side, and entered the rainbow realm. Again and again, I have expanded my heart, and found enormous gratitude and peace within myself regardless of the circumstances. And I know I am not even listing everything, here. I feel like I am overflowing. All of you have been guiding me in the most beautiful way. I have felt incredibly loved and supported during this entire journey. And now I want to share all of this love, pass on these precious gifts you have been giving me. Maybe I can be a guide for others, too. I feel ready for that."

Once again, I remember all the people in the castle garden. It seems so long ago that I was so excited to meet them, curious who they were and what they were about. Somehow that never happened….

"You were not quite ready," KenLa answers my musings with a loving smile. "You had to complete all parts of this particular journey first, before you could become a guide for others. But you are ready now, and I am happy to hear that you are choosing to share what you have learned."

"I am curious though, KenLa," I think out loud. "I just said that I wanted to go out into the real world. The people in the castle garden aren't the 'real world' — or are they?"

*Hmmm, this is becoming interesting.... My book character is musing about the real world :)! And YES! I want to know how we get to weave this energetic dreamworld into real life, into real physical experiences, how to close the gap. Gap . . . that makes me think of how my book character crossed the impossible chasm in front of the "Chapel of my Dreams" — changing her perspective and trusting.*

"Allowing" is the word appearing in front of me. "Allowing".... This does not really answer my question, but I am sure it will be answered soon enough.

*Soon enough! One of my affirmation cards (which reminds me that it would be a great idea to start doing them daily, again) reads: "My life flows with divine timing." I have learned to trust in that (most of the time), and it actually feels like it does flow with divine timing.*

Right now, it feels like my wish to bring all this information into the real world has opened a floodgate of energy and emotions that I need to expand into, ground, be present with and, yes, allow! Breathing, opening, being, grounding, surrendering to what wants to move through me without needing to really explain or change it — my main focus on expanding, especially my heart. Making space for all these "real" people — with all their stories, history, and energies — to enter my world.

After a while, I feel more like my usual self again, in a both-feet-on-the-ground-let's-do-this kind of way — but with my heart, which feels like it is smiling, wide open. I notice a clarity that feels solid, grounded *and* expanded at the same time. I turn again to KenLa, who has been sitting close by, a calm and patient presence. "This feels really good, KenLa, almost as if I am beginning to bridge those two worlds. Am I?" I ask.

"What do you know?" comes the calm answer. He sounds peaceful, and at the same time slightly removed, as if he wants to stay in the background and not disturb my own discoveries. As if he's leaving it up to me to be the leader.

When I check back in with myself, it feels like I have entered a space of happy, colorful creation. I see bright spirals, waves, circles, swirls, Merkabahs, and other geometric shapes vividly filling a space in front of my eyes, in bold shades that are moving, dancing, weaving, intermingling. Some of this I can see, and some I can only feel. This creative expanse feels incredibly joyful and happy, and is in perpetual motion. What am I looking at? I somehow *know* that this is a creative space. Are these my creations? What if this space and its creative power originate in the Rainbow Realm, but reach into "real" life?

I become aware of a bright light within my heart. A guiding light? It feels like it. If it is, where is it leading me? It seems like it's literally becoming a lantern, illuminating the path in front of me. Like it is shining on the inside and projecting its radiance to a spot in front of my eyes so I can see it. I feel like that deep-sea creature, the anglerfish, minus the scary teeth. (Although my teeth *have* been getting a bit crooked in the last few years.) This thought makes me laugh, which seems to make the lantern shine brighter.

This is exciting! I am eager to know where it wants to lead me. But my eagerness does not yield any results. The lantern simply dangles in front of my inner eyes without any prompt to go anywhere, do anything. Hmmm, that's curious.... I wonder....

Switching from eagerness to curiosity feels like taking an internal step backwards. Like taking the car out of gear and waiting for directions, instead of sitting in the driveway like an overexcited racehorse. So I thank that guiding light for being there. Even if it is not leading me anywhere right now, it is illuminating the gift of my present space. As a result of my gratitude, I begin feeling a sweetness emanating from this light. We have seemingly opened a channel of connection and communication that was not there before, despite the fact that it is my own heart's projection. The urgency has evaporated, and I am simply basking in the light, feeling my heart being illuminated, thinking there will be guidance when it is time for guidance.

I can trust my own heart, can't I? Yes, I can. My heart has never led me wrong. I might not have been aware of its guiding light, but whenever I was able to hear its whispers and feel its nudges, it has always steered me in the most loving, albeit sometimes unusual, direction. So YES! I can trust my own heart.

After a while, the light in front of me gets brighter, and I also notice a pull forward that seems to be coming directly from my heart — as if it has put itself into gear and I am being nudged forward. I smile at KenLa, who still rests peacefully beside me. "Looks like it is time to start moving," I tell him. "Are you coming?"

"Actually, my job as your guide is done. It is time for you to begin exploring on your own, so you learn how to perceive the guidance of your heart even more clearly," he says, returning my smile. "You have learned many lessons, had many insights and revelations, and received many tools. Now you are essentially becoming your own guide and a guide for others. However, there will always be many beings and angels surrounding you, ready and happy to assist. So remember to ask for help when you need it."

Wow, I am not sure I am ready for this — but the pull of my heart is getting stronger by the second, and I can neither ignore nor resist it much longer. "Thank you, KenLa," I say with tears in my eyes. I am overflowing with gratitude for KenLa and everyone else who has assisted me on this wondrous journey. "Can I give you a hug good-bye?"

Claudia Sasse

We both get up from our seats and I take a step towards KenLa — until I find myself also standing on the water, which somehow does not surprise me. When we embrace, it feels like my heart is simultaneously exploding and beginning to tune into an even higher, finer frequency. I feel KenLa's beautiful, peace-filled heart plus everyone I have ever known and will ever know. It seems like I am embracing the world. We are standing there in presence, heart-to-heart in this beautiful exchange, in a moment beyond time.

When we pull apart, KenLa takes the Pipe of Truth from his side and solemnly presents it to me with both hands and a slight bow of his head. "Allow this holy pipe to assist you in guiding you on the sacred path of your own truth and supporting others with the same. It will not wear you down but will be there whenever you call on it."

I feel moved, honored, and full of respect when I silently hold out my hands and bow my head to receive the beautiful instrument. When the pipe touches them, I am surprised how at home I feel with it, as if it belongs there in my hands.

I know it is time to leave — and when I turn to go, the pipe vanishes so that I won't have to carry it. Instead, all I notice is my own lightness and the lightness of my luminous, shimmery dress. I look back at KenLa and wave before I take the first step, following my guiding light on the water towards the middle of the pool. I take a deep breath and smile. And with the next step I find myself back out on the wide-open mountainside.

First moments out in the open air
Breathing in freedom
Breathing out uncertainty
New legs still wobbly
Will they carry me?
Only the next step will tell
And the one after that
As I keep on walking

# 22

Oh wow! That was instant. I guess my heart knew where I needed to go next. Does this mean I just bridged the Rainbow Dimension and the real world? Hmmm, I guess I shall find out. I notice some women and children walking towards me. They look strangely familiar. As they come closer, I can see why — they are all younger versions of myself. I see:
a girl carrying her roller skates,
a little two-year-old eager to discover the world,
the cigarette-smoking teenager,
the twenty-something traveling the world,
the bride,
the new mother,
the friend,
the daughter,
the wife,
living in different places,
doing different kinds of work,
having different kinds of friends,
the explorer and student of consciousness,
the adventurer setting out into a new life.
I see a happy version, a sad version, a stuck version, a free version, heavier and skinnier versions, open and closed-off versions.
My first reaction to them varies from "Oh-I-wish-I-could-live-that-life-again" to "I'm-so-happy-I'll-never-have-to-live-through-that-again." Some versions I even reject, while I quite approve of others, as all of them walk steadily towards me. It feels like there is something here for me to take a closer look at, but this whole scene is moving too fast and I need to create some space to take it all in. I raise my hand and

command, "Stop!" And the whole scene actually comes to a halt — almost as if I have created an assembly of wax figures on the grass on the mountainside.

I walk towards the figure closest to me. It's me dancing and smiling at a New Year's Eve party in 2008. I look carefree, relaxed, happy, and at home there. This *is* actually at my relatively new home, celebrating with my relatively new friends. When I lightly touch the figure, she comes to life again. Slightly out of breath, beautiful, vibrant, smiling brightly, inviting me to celebrate with her.

Yes, I'd like to celebrate. I'd like to look younger again, but I also know that this is not about reentering a world that I have already left behind. *So what* am *I to do with all this?* I wonder.

So... this is me! This is *all* me. And I kind of know that it's about gratitude and loving all these different versions of me as the ones that brought me here — to this point. Except, if I am honest, right now I actually *don't* want to be at the point where I am at. I really, really want to be my younger version again — but I also don't want to give up my present knowing, and my beautiful space on the mountainside.

This is getting really muddled and confusing. I need to create more space again. I take a few steps back, sit down on the grass, and look past all the figures at the wide expanse of the ocean, breathing, feeling the air inflate my lungs. I turn up my face towards the sun and feel the warm sunshine on my skin. The grass tickles my legs, wildflowers sway in the breeze, and some insects buzz around me. The whole hill is alive. I am ALIVE! I breathe all this aliveness into my heart, and feel my heart lighting up again.

And a knowing opens up deep down inside that I could not possibly be in a more perfect spot — looking the way I look, feeling the way I feel, experiencing what I experience, knowing what I know, doing what I do. *And*, I actually can't screw this up — this thing called my life. But I *can* make it even more beautiful. For now, it is about loving and celebrating all

Claudia Sasse

these different versions of me as the ones that brought me here — to this perfect space in time.

I don't feel like leaving my present vantage point on the mountainside any more, but I still want to meet my former selves. I would like to invite them over to join me in my present space. I look at my New Year's party self and wave at her to come over to me. What a gift that I actually get to be with myself! Her radiance and ease of being is contagious, and I feel instantly lighter. We are having a bit of a dance party, and after a while I thank her. When I give her a hug, she dissolves into my present form. One by one, I make my former selves come to life again simply by putting my attention on their figure and inviting them to come over to me.

I laugh with them, I cry with them, I have compassion, I comfort them, I cheer them on, I am proud of them and I admire them — but mostly, I love them deeply and unconditionally as they, one by one, integrate back into my present form. In the end, there is only one girl left, sitting cross-legged, tucked away in a shadowy spot surrounded by some bushes. She has come to life, but her head is hanging low so she does not see me waving her over to my spot. I actually don't even quite recognize her, but she looks sad somehow. So I walk over to her and sit down across from her.

"Hi, how are you? Would you like to join me over there at my spot in the sun?" I ask.

When she lifts her head, I almost fall backwards. Her eyes are catlike, yellow, and bloodshot. She has fangs and hisses at me. I have not seen many horror movies, but she definitely looks like a creature out of one of them.

Whoa, what am I supposed to do with *that*? She hangs her head again. She does not feel menacing to me, just sad somehow — and stuck.

"I can't come to you over there. Nobody wants to see me. I scare people. I scare *you*! I have to stay here so I won't do any harm," she says, sounding sad and hopeless.

My heart goes out to her. "Yes, I admit, you took me by surprise. And I also admit that I probably did not want to see you or be with you for most of my life. But I want to see you now. I want to be with you now. I'd love to do this in that spot over there in the sun where I just came from, though. Would that be ok? I promise there is enough space around so you could freak out and go crazy without harming anyone."

"Ok…," she says hesitantly. But when she looks up this time, her features look more relaxed and her eyes less bloodshot and catlike. You can even see a hint of blue in them.

"Come with me," I say, as I get up and hold out my hand towards her. She takes it and reluctantly stands up, her head still hanging low. Yet as we begin walking hand-in-hand towards my sunny spot on the grass, she begins looking around, taking in the bright spaciousness and beautiful vistas. By the time we get to my favorite spot, she has turned into a bright-eyed, curious, and excited girl, laughing and bouncing up and down.

"Come sit with me," I invite her. "What happened to you? I mean, before I saw you today, what happened to you?"

The girl sits down next to me, legs outstretched, leaning back on her hands, taking in the view, and the sunshine, and smiles.

"It feels so good to be out in the open again. It's so free and so light." A shadow crosses over her face as she continues, "I wanted to do something fun like this — go outside and play with my friends, when my little brother clung to my leg and tried to stop me. I totally freaked out, turned into the creature you saw earlier, and almost threw him down the stairs." A slight shadow begins to envelop her as she speaks.

Yes, I remember that moment. It made me decide to do my very best not to ever get really angry again.

"Hmmm, so you have the capacity to turn into a monster, just like Dr. Jekyll and Mr. Hyde," I state neutrally.

I am not sure what to do with this. Am I supposed to love this part of me? Forgive myself? It's definitely an uneasy

Claudia Sasse

feeling to think I might do this whenever cornered. The little girl must be sensing my unease, and the slight shadow that started enveloping her as she shared her story is becoming stronger again, her soft features harder. "Wait! I'm sorry," I say. "I really, really want to be with you — both sides of you. Can you show me?"

Scenes begin to flood in, gruesome scenes that go way beyond my experiences in this life — torture, murder, mutilation.

"I know how to do all this," the little girl says, "but I don't want to, so I am keeping myself locked away."

I am simply being present with all of it and ask her, "Is there more you want to show me?" I am shown a prison scene. A different version of her in a grown-up male body is just being released from prison, longing for the simple pleasures of a free life. The man turns, looks straight at me with intensely blue eyes and says, "All my horrible deeds were done out of fear and lack. There seemed to be no other way out. Often, I have justified them, and sometimes they have even turned me on. However, you have been practicing and choosing a different kind of way, a new abundant kind of way — living through your heart. This choice, your willingness to be present and to see me, is releasing me from my self-imposed prison. Thank you!"

I turn to the little girl solemnly sitting next to me. The shadows are gone, and so is any hardness in her features. She looks innocent and sweet, with her hair softly blowing in the breeze. "Do you think you are free to be out in the sunshine, now?" I ask.

"Yes, I think I am," she answers with a big, beaming, brilliant smile. We hug each other for a long while before she integrates back into me.

Through the haze of the eternal struggles of the mind
Love's voice beckons
Join my flow and leave the struggles behind
Allow yourself to be carried by me

# 23

"It's all right here in your heart," I hear, sitting on the grass by myself, a bit lost as to what to do next. Ah yes, follow the pull of my heart. Except that after the integration, I cannot feel it as strongly as before. Actually, I am not feeling a pull at all. But if what I have just heard is true (and after everything I've experienced, I'm quite sure it is), it is indeed *all* right here in my heart. Gently, I dial back my expectations, slight impatience, and sudden sense of urgency, and simply sit quietly and connect my breath to my heart.

I receive an inner picture of lots of junk. I am wading through it. There are mostly metal parts of some sort. Why? I don't know. Next, I see a little makeshift town in the California desert I once visited that was mostly built out of junk reimagined into art. While I appreciated how people had turned trash into treasures, being there made me feel uneasy. Maybe it also had something to do with all the drug abuse still lingering in that space, or maybe it was just all the old rusty decaying stuff. That image is a stark contrast to the beautiful, abundantly green, fresh, clear, expansive, open space I find myself in right now.

The scene keeps evolving, though, and one of the inhabitants of the desert town turns towards me and looks at me with intense eyes. "This is *not* your place, and you don't ever have to even remotely like it, work on improving it, and definitely not adapt to it. This feels like home to *us*. It is *your* job to fully inhabit and illuminate that which feels like home to *you*. Work with that, improve that, create more beauty there, love *that*."

I nod in acknowledgment and respect. I am grateful for the reminder that I am not here to change anybody's world

— unless they want to change it themselves and ask for assistance — but mainly I am here to create my own beautiful world, with an open invitation for others to visit or join me.

I go back to breathing into my heart. And I begin seeing a beautiful flower garden starting to grow inside and around it. It reminds me of my Secret Garden.

*I'm recalling something my friend Melissa mentioned yesterday about not only using my energy but also connecting to the Universal energy. While this concept is certainly not new to me, this time it landed in a completely different way.*

My fictitious self and my real self are flowing into each other more and more, now. I consciously ask to be connected to the Universal energy, and instantaneously I see-feel connected to a bright stream of light entering my head and completely enveloping me. My inner light grows simultaneously, and I see-feel it expanding way beyond my present form. Next, I connect to Gaia — specifically, to the incredibly rich and fertile land I am currently sitting on. It feels like the land is anchoring all this light — giving it substance.

As I keep softly breathing into my heart, something begins happening that I don't have to actively facilitate at all. I am simply witnessing it. I am seeing-feeling many new aspects of myself being integrated and activated:

The earthy healer,

the brilliant sovereign queen,

the charismatic public speaker who is almost ready to come out of the shadows,

the connector,

the peacemaker,

the activator,

the explorer of new possibilities,

the happily relaxed mother, and even grandmother, peacefully and joyfully settled in her home,

and the deeply connected ecstatic lover and co-creator —
all firmly rooted in Gaia and connected to Spirit.

An awareness comes quietly and without fanfare — matter-
of-fact, really — in an "of course" kind of way:

I AM READY. IT IS TIME.

Love All.

# 24

---

I get up from the lawn and start down the slope. As I begin to walk, I can feel the pull of my heart again. It is not intense now, more matter-of-fact — just like the awareness, earlier, that I am ready. My heart is leading me over to the left. I see a group of four women, all dressed in white, sitting by a tree in the soft golden sunshine. When I approach them, one of them stands up, turns towards me, and stretches out her arms with a warm smile. "Please join us," she invites me. "We have been trying to solve the problem of these nuts. Many of them are shriveled and dry. Also... there aren't enough of them."

I see four slightly shriveled dark-brown nuts lying on the ground among the four women. I like the women's energy. It feels very soft, welcoming, and loving. I nod and smile at them, grateful for the sweet space they have created. The nuts remind me of kukui nuts. Kukui is the state tree of the Hawaiian Islands, and represents protection, peace, enlightenment, and light. Its oil-rich nuts have a multitude of uses. But I'm actually not quite sure what those nuts are. And I also wonder what *my* role is, here.

When I check into my heart, it becomes clear that while I very much resonate with the energy of these women, I cannot contribute much besides creating space for finding new solutions. As much as I love and appreciate nature and plants, they are not really my expertise. Although I would like to join their circle, it feels that instead I am being pulled somewhere that feels more naturally aligned for me. And yet I feel deep respect and gratitude for their efforts around an issue that seems important not only for them but also for many other people, even all of humanity. So I thank them sincerely for their service and for welcoming me so openly. I ask for their work to be truly blessed and divinely guided. I also leave them with a question that often opens up new solutions: "What else is possible?" and promise to send a plant expert their way, should I encounter one.

"Thank you for the awareness that, while I very much respect and like these women, this subject is not for me to get deeply involved in." I address this universal thought of gratitude to no one in particular as I head on. It reminds me of all my angel and other multidimensional friends, though, and so I ask them to join me on my path for the pure joy of the experience and to be of assistance, if they wish. I instantaneously feel them in my heart and all around me, although I cannot really see any of them. It seems like my book character is merging more and more with my regular human self and the world of my normal sensory experiences.

I remember how excited I was, a while ago, by the opportunity to meet all the people I saw in the castle garden and on this mountainside; but that hasn't really happened yet. I muse that maybe I had to learn all the lessons and have all these incredible experiences first, in order to be able to really be present with them. While I might not be much of a plant expert, I LOVE people.

I see a young woman coming my way. She looks absolutely beautiful. But her beauty is beyond simple physical beauty: she glows from the inside out. It's as if she is effortlessly walking within her own source of light, which illuminates the space around her. She is wearing a flowing white summer dress, her long golden hair moving weightlessly in the light breeze. She seems enthralled by the natural beauty around her, and when she notices me she flashes me the brightest smile.

"Hello," I greet her, beaming back at her. "Who are you?"

She chuckles. "Are you sure you want to know?"

"Yes," I laugh, "I am sure."

"Do you promise that you will believe me and not fight me when I tell you?" she says, with just the smallest hint of seriousness in her clear, sparkling eyes.

"Yes, I promise," I reply. I'm quite curious and slightly confused by now. Why would I fight her?

"I am you. I am how you appear in the world when you are fully present, connected, grounded, and with your heart fully open."

I begin my protest: "Well, for starters, I am clearly neither as young nor as beautiful as you are—" And then I stop. I had promised not to fight her.

She looks at me amused, with slightly raised eyebrows, and then relaxes her face into a sweet, kind smile.

"Will you receive this?" she asks simply.

Will I receive this…? An internal argument starts gaining momentum. *"I guess I* can't *stop fighting, after all. I cannot possibly be this beautiful, radiant, and charismatic. It would be conceited of me to think so. Aren't I supposed to be humble? But what if she is right?"* I can't stop smiling at that thought. *"And what if I could actually see that and activate that in others — that the more I shine, the more others get to shine, as well? It already kind of happened in the castle garden, didn't it?"* That thought makes me smile even more.

"Ok," I consent, "I believe you."

"Oh good, it is time," is all she says before she integrates.

I feel light and buoyant, and my heart pulls me to walk further down the mountain until I hit the road below. I begin walking to the right, towards Pololū Valley. It feels as if I am walking towards the real thing, not an imaginary place but the place that I know from my frequent hikes. Usually, I drive this part of the road in my car, so walking along here is new. I can feel the strong pull of my heart towards the valley, met with an equally strong signal towards me from down there.

*This is not imaginary, anymore. I am feeling the strongest urge to physically do what I am writing about. It is early, only about 6:00 in the morning. I close my laptop, grab a bottle of water, hop in the car, and drive towards that place. I park right by the sign that advertises 485 acres for sale on the mauka (mountain) side, then put on my walking shoes and set off. This stretch of road, which I have driven so often, feels completely different on foot.*

*The air is a perfect temperature, balmy. The light breeze gently lifts my hair in a gravity-defying way. Morning clouds lend an additional element of depth to the grassy, richly green tree-dotted hillside. Trees of all varieties, some bearing fruit, abundantly line the street. There are guavas, citrus, papayas, and ulu (breadfruit) ripening on them. Horses are grazing in pastures — one looks at me from behind a hedge, picture-perfectly framed by a rainbow of delicate flowers. On the ocean side, the sun is breaking through the clouds, creating a bright island of light on the water. The air is fragrant with the sweet smell of blossoms and fruit. A stately tree with narrow leaves (maybe eucalyptus?) calls for my attention, communicating with me on a deep level. The street undulates on, with slight curves and little hills.*

*I notice an enormously tall mango tree shedding its sweet juicy fruit next to a gurgling stream, but I have nothing to peel them with. But then, a few yards later, I am gifted with a fresh, ripe guava on the side of the road instead. I bite into it, tasting the sweet, slightly tart flesh, while the morning breeze softly caresses my skin and the wind plays a symphony in the crowns of the trees. I am in the midst of a sensory feast, with an overflow of abundance and sweetness all around me.*

*This morning walk feels different than any I have ever taken. It feels deeper, richer — as if I am literally walking through different dimensions at the same time. I feel intensely present, fully receiving what is being gifted to me.*

Claudia Sasse

*Just by the old mule station, the steep, lush coastline becomes visible on the left, with its waterfall and little islands. Seeing it appear while moving at this slower pace takes my breath away with its beauty. A few yards later, I get to savor the wide drop of the valley opening up in front of my eyes. When I reach the rocky path that descends to the bottom, I take off my shoes. I always walk this trail barefoot, soaking up the grounding energy of the land. Because I am being protective of a toe I had stubbed the night before, I walk much more mindfully than my usual skip-and-hop down the smooth lava rocks.*

*This path is so familiar to me by now. I actually had powered up the hill in the fading evening light less than twelve hours ago. Yet this morning, it feels like I am being enfolded by a different world, one that is integrating the different dimensions I have been writing about into the "real world" as I've known it so far. The sound of the crashing waves wafting up to my ears seems a curiously foreign element in my present visuals of trees, dirt, and rocks, until the view opens up to reveal the drop off to the ocean below.*

*I know the veils are thin down in the valley, so I almost expect to physically see "my guys" when I get there — Laura, C, J, 153, KenLa, my angel friends, and all the other guides and beings. But when I reach the bottom floor, everything looks pretty much the way it usually does. I am guided to sit on the long trunk of a fallen tree. When I turn to the right, I see the river and the green valley sprawled out in front of me; straight ahead, across the river, is the embankment of the ironwood-covered hill, with the root that looks like a buffalo down by the water; and to my left, the strong waves continuously roll onto the black-sand beach. I've sat here a couple of times, but usually I choose a different tree, closer to the water.*

*I turn towards the sweet green backside of the valley. It's being made quite clear to me to leave my phone in my backpack — no pictures, no videos today. "This is your time,"*

I hear. "Just *be*, feel, and receive. This is *your* integration time. This particular journey is coming to an end." *Laura in her pink jacket briefly pops up in front of my inner eyes, but otherwise not much is happening that I am aware of. After the wild journey in the book and the multidimensional walk down here, I definitely expected something more unusual — more fanfare, more excitement. But things couldn't feel more normal. At one point, I notice the sensation of wearing phantom glasses across the bridge of my nose that I sometimes have. I've yet to figure out what that means. Am I to do something with that?* "Just feel it," *I hear, and after a while the pressure lessens.*

*Otherwise I am simply being, breathing, feeling, opening, and trusting that I am receiving whatever I need to receive. I am not really feeling all that much different, though, to be honest. After a while, the energy shifts. I sense that it is about time to go back up the hill. I feel at peace and activated at the same time. And a knowing begins to fill the space, expanding within me:*

I AM HOME! I AM FREE! AND I AM
READY TO MEET THE WORLD!

# THE JOURNEY CONTINUES

*I find myself on the "helipad." To me, the helipad is a step on the stairway to heaven. Outwardly it is nothing special — a wide lava field about three miles below the Mauna Kea summit. For some of us, though, it is filled with otherworldly wonder and beings. It can be experienced as a full-spectrum gateway into other dimensions, allowing pieces of remembrance of our wholeness — of who we really are — to come back to us. It can make you feel completely high with wildly expansive energies, or creep you out if you are not quite tuned into the higher frequencies of the place. For me, I feel mostly a grounded multidimensional expansion. The last time I was there a few days ago, it felt like entering a communion of sorts with Pleiadian beings, helping me to ground my heart.*

*So now I find myself back on the helipad. This time, I am not physically there, but have been asked to "travel" there energetically. As I notice a ring of light slightly off to the right, in front the wall of piled rock that intersects the field, I also am asked to begin writing.*

*Well, here we are! I am writing and I am curious about what is to unfold.*

"Dear Ones." I hear a sweet yet powerful voice echoing out from inside the ring of light (something between a ring of pure light and a ring of fire).

"Dear Ones," the voice repeats, "we have asked you to gather in this place, even if only in your energy bodies, to bring you a message. As you find your way to these words, you become part of the gathering. It is time to surrender into the softness of your beingness. It is time to surrender effort. It is time to surrender opposition. It is time to surrender righteousness, expectation, and judgment. It is time to feel yourself as part of the whole.

Dear Ones, there is no reason to be afraid of this. You might feel like you are being asked to surrender the weapons and defenses that you have needed for your survival until now. Yet we ask you to consider that every time you hurt another being, you are essentially only hurting yourself. Whenever you put up your defenses, you block connection and flow. You are part of the whole; so whenever any facet of that whole is injured, you are injured. Whenever any part is blocked off, you are being blocked. And whenever any part of that whole is loved, you are being loved.

So ask, 'How can I love more? How can I be the space for others to heal? How can I meet everyone with respect, even if I don't agree with them? How can I build someone up instead of tearing them down? How can I see beyond their story and their behavior into the purity of their heart?'

Beloveds, you are at a crossroads, and you might have heard, said, or even felt this many times, recently. So honor that you are at a crossroads!"

I have not paid much attention to the ring of light, but instead focused on capturing the words. When I refocus on the ring, I still find myself outside of it, looking in. Suddenly, I can see the outlines of what appears to be a tall female figure. She raises her arms, and the light flames that have been hovering close to the ground shoot up and become a wall of fiery white-golden light. I can see the figure twirling in the middle of the light, holding something like a magic wand in each hand. The walls, which were straight, begin spinning around her like a tornado. While this looks like a nice bit of magic, I wonder, "What is the point?"

I hear light, pearly laughter in response from inside the spinning firelight spiral. "Come inside and you'll find out."

Hmmm, can I just walk through? The spinning and the fire bit are a little concerning, but I decide to follow that voice anyway. Plus, obviously, I am not there in my "real" body :)

Here I go — and my sense of adventure must have kicked in, because I am definitely more intrigued than fearful. I take a deep breath and walk towards the firelight wall, careful not to twist my ankle on the many lava rocks in the field. And why would that even matter to my energy body?

I am slightly amused by my thoughts, when I begin feeling the effects of the swirling tornado of light. There is a soft, refreshing coolness that feels more like a gentle breeze than a forceful wind. As I walk closer, the spinning wall of firelight easily gives way and I move through a layer of what I can best describe as "light information," which seems to have way more depth than its initial appearance would suggest. The color is still white and gold, and within these colors there is code, and some sort of language that my intellect does not grasp but my heart fully understands. I am moving through a world that looks somewhat three-dimensional to my eyes, yet I can feel how I am being enveloped by infinitely more dimensions.

I can't think my way through, here. I can only "be" my way through, here. And what does that even mean? Except that I know exactly what it means. Breathing deeply, expanding, feeling my body, feeling my heart both as part of my body and as a gateway to all the other realms and dimensions. My feet are magnetically rooted to the lava floor, which feels smooth now, no big rocks to stumble over. I keep breathing deeply, opening, opening, opening to absorb all of the information. A silly grin must be plastered on my face. Why? No idea. Just feeling a rich, beautiful light complexity that is also incredibly simple and clear. All this makes me excited and giddy, somehow.

I begin thinking about money. Money, of all things! Really? Historically, I have not been the best at earning it through any of my professions, and yet I have always been provided for, supported, gifted — sometimes unexpectedly and seemingly out of nowhere. Recently, instead of having fixed rates for my work, I have been guided to invite my clients to pay whatever makes them feel happy and grateful. Hmmm, how do these thoughts fit in here?

I am still moving through the firelight wall, and only now does it even occur to me that I can detect no spinning sensation while walking through. However, there is no end in sight. Will I ever make it to the center of the circle?

My surroundings have changed, and now I am in a maze of mirrors. I keep seeing myself in all kinds of ways, but there is no clear path. I am feeling a little lost, and this is beginning to creep me out. I stop to try and gather myself into presence and beingness again. Breathing deeply, feeling my feet on the ground, feeling my connection to spirit, feeling my heart. I know the invitation was benevolent, loving. The voice sweet, talking about surrendering opposition and defense.

Wait, was I actually sweet-talked into putting down my defenses, doing something that will ultimately hurt me? WTF! When my mind throws in this thought, a slight panic sets in. As the panic grows, the light dims and the mirrors change, revealing sharp, pointy edges. My reflection becomes distorted. The scene is scary, menacing; but through waves of panic comes a quiet, soft voice of remembrance: "The power lies within you. Nobody can take that away from you. The truth lives in your heart. You can always connect to it."

And in the middle of this maze of cutting glass, distortion, and dimming light, I sit down and really focus on breathing into my heart, connecting to its wisdom. Will it tell me I am in the right place? Or will it reveal that I was gullible?

When I can feel no concern and only softness in my heart, I relax into that — surrendering, trusting. I feel like I am being cradled in my deepest, sweetest, ultimate home space. The darkness gives way to a luminous, soft, golden light. The mirrors round their edges, and I notice a thin golden thread on the ground 90 degrees to my left, playfully vanishing behind a corner. I get up and curiously pick up the thread. Will it guide me? I check in with my heart, and all I can feel is a joyfully happy "YES!"

I start walking through the maze of mirrors again, winding the thread into a ball. I used to knit, so this feels quite familiar. What gets reflected back to me is not only my regular self, but also scenes from my life, people, places, events — past, present, and, seemingly, future. All those scenes are happy, peaceful, and . . sweet: there is that word, again. The whole thing is delightful — full of light. I keep winding up the thread; and before I know it, I step through an opening into the circle with a big ball of precious golden thread in my hands.

In the center of the circle is a white, luminous, sparkling figure. It is so tiny, though, that it makes me feel like a giant. "Hello," I say as I enter the space. "It was you who spoke earlier, and who created the wall of firelight, wasn't it? You appeared quite tall. then. How come you are so tiny now?"

"It isn't I who have shrunk, it is you who has grown," she answers, radiating a sweet smile my way. "I always appear as tall as I choose to. Come." And she beckons for me to join her in the middle of the circle.

As I approach her, I notice how the walls of the maze I just stepped out of vanish. And when I reach the center, all I can see is a wide-open, luminous expanse bathed in white-golden light. It looks like the lava field that I know, and at the same time like a place I have never been before. It looks dreamy, yet substantial — manifested light or an open field of possibilities.

When I turn back towards the beautiful figure, I am at eye-level with her. Have I shrunk or has she grown? Does it matter?

She laughs; and there is so much warmth, ease, and lightness in her laughter that it blows my heart wide open. I LOVE her! I have no idea who she is, but I love her so much! There is a connection, a bond that flows from my heart to hers and back — feather-light, yet getting stronger by the second. "Who are you?" I ask her.

"I am you, and you are me," she answers, her laughter pearls ringing lightly in the air. I don't quite understand, but I can feel how all my energy centers are being activated. I want to meld with her, become one with her. Feel her as part of me. Feel myself as part of her.

And then I do.

"This is the Oneness that you are seeking," she tells me, "but that you are also so afraid of on this planet. Isn't it indescribably beautiful?"

I'm in rapture. "Yes, it is!" I say. Through this profound connection, I am seeing what she sees, knowing what she knows. Our hearts are dancing around each other. I can feel a deep peacefulness; and simultaneously, my heart is bursting with excitement.

And a whole new world opens up. I see happiness and laughter. People moving about freely, joyfully, often purposefully. There is an incredible ease and lightness in the air. Once in a while, people meld with each other, the way she and I just melded together, their love for each other and the world around them creating new life in all forms: energy forms, babies, community projects, events, buildings, art, gardens…. Or they simply enjoy the incredible sensation of being in unity with each other.

I can also see the process of melding together occurring within groups of three or more people. It's an eternal dance of finding each other and letting go again — from the spaciousness of relishing one's sovereignty in a whole and sacred way, to the ecstasy of a complete union, or the joyful, flowing exchange of deep yet spacious connection — inhaling and exhaling. While I can't really make out faces or specifics, everything feels and looks much lighter than what I am used to in my regular life. But it also has so much more substance and depth.

Claudia Sasse

"You will experience your life more and more like this as your journey continues," she explains, "after you have fully come home to yourself, left the heavy backpack of your fears, defenses, and judgments behind, and set out on your new adventure curious and unburdened." She continues, "Not all of you will choose to do this, and you need to respect that, but you can choose this path if you want to.

That is the crossroads. The possibility of a New Earth experience has opened up, as there are enough of you on the planet by now who are choosing a new way of being. You have reached the critical mass, the tipping point, to be able to create a new reality. 'For the entire planet?' you ask." That was just what I had been thinking. "Yes, eventually," she assures me. "Initially it will be more like you are existing in two different worlds side by side, until the experience of New Earth and unity consciousness will become 'mainstream' and any remaining fear-based behavior will simply fall away."

Whoa, this is absolutely amazing. "What can I do to facilitate this, speed it up, experience it in my real life?" I want to know. "Initially, you were addressing many of us. How can we invite them here?" And then that piece about money flashed in. "What are we doing with that?" The questions spill out of me. And while I am connected to her knowing, I cannot quite discern, yet, the concrete answers that my mind craves. I guess there are different ways or focal points of being in unity that I still have to learn.

She laughs again, the fairy-feather-light sound playing in my ears, caressing my soul. "You want to know the first secret for living in this world more and more?" she asks in a sweetly flirtatious way.

"Yes, please!" I answer eagerly.

"Breathe!!" she laughs. "Breathe yourself into presence, into wholeness. Breathe into your heart. Let your breath connect you to your powerful planet as well as to the expanse of Source and all that is. In addition, you have collected all the important tools you might need on your recent journey home. Simply use your breath to soften into remembering."

"What about the others? How will your words from before reach them? How will this entire book reach them, actually?" The questions tumble out of me eagerly.

"Firstly, your entire being serves as a vibrational invitation into this world—as you share your message, have conversations, or simply smile at people in passing. And of course it gets amplified during your sessions and group events. The more you open up, the more this will become part of who you are, and the more you will radiate it outward as a ripple of light that will attract people just as you were attracted to me without knowing anything about me, not even my name. It is SUN, by the way," she beams.

"You can also ask for assistance. There are beings of light in all dimensions who would be beyond happy to help. But you already know that, don't you?" The love that flows out of her eyes as she says this almost brings me to tears.

"Lastly, stay curious. Ask joy-filled, light-hearted questions: 'How can I invite all the members of my soul family who are ready to hear, live, be this? How can I expand my reach in the most joyful, fun, and exciting way?' Also, ask the book itself, as it is its own being/life form: 'How can I bring you out into the light? How can I serve you? How can we expand this even more?' And of course there is your trusted, 'What else is possible?'" she says with a wink.

I notice how I am furrowing my eyebrows, trying to remember all this correctly and do it "right." She notices my strain and says, "Relax and breathe lightness into all of this. You are abundantly supported. You do, and always will, have everything you need, and more. You cannot mess this up. It is only a matter of how easy and joyful you choose for your experience to be."

"What about that whole money question?" I ask quickly when I notice her presence becoming weaker.

"Stay open and curious," I hear. "Something new is unfolding; but this is not my expertise. You will learn more about it on your journey ahead. Maybe you will even write another book about it ;)"

I can feel her loving, flirtatious wink more than I can see it as she fades out of my energy field, leaving me filled up with love that's overflowing and immensely spacious at the same time.

Yes, maybe there will be another book; but for now, I am so happy that I got to write this one, and that you got to read it. And I am tremendously happy and grateful that we are part of each other's soul family and found each other.

WITH AN ABUNDANCE OF LOVE FROM MY HEART TO YOURS.

xoxo Claudia

# LET'S KEEP PLAYING

WEBSITE
Visit me at my online home for FREE LightCode
activations, events and other goodies :)
www.ClaudiaSasse.com

PRIVATE READINGS AND ACTIVATIONS
Schedule a 30-minute "Igniting Possibilities"
session:
https://tinyurl.com/IgnitingPossibilities   (As
space allows)
Here is what others are saying: www.
ClaudiaSasse.com/client-love/

SPEAKING - PODCASTS - EVENTS
I love to open spaces of possibilities, expansion, transformation
and magic during podcasts and events. Let's talk! You can
reach me at: claudia@claudiasasse.com

RETREATS
And then there is always the possibility of a
magical, transformational retreat in paradise
:) Come visit me on the Big Island of Hawaii!
Schedule an exploration chat, if that thought
makes your heart sing. https://tinyurl.com/
ExplorationChat

PRIVATE FACEBOOK GROUP
Join our HeartLight Women's Leadership Circle
that is mentioned on the very first page.
https://www.facebook.com/groups/
heartlightleadership/

SHARE YOUR THOUGHTS
How was your experience with LoveBytes? I'd LOVE to hear
from you. Drop me a line at: claudia@claudiasasse.com

# ABOUT THE AUTHOR

Claudia is a New Earth career guide, heart-centered visionary intuitive, and catalyst for light-filled transformation. One of her greatest joys is supporting her multi-talented clients to channel the wholeness of who they are into meaningful, joy-filled work that not only changes the world but also nourishes their soul.

She uses her multiple claire-sensory gifts and her down-to-earth practicality to help them build the energetic foundation, create the framework, and discover the golden thread that allow them to move forward with their life/soul mission with clarity, ease, and confidence — often thriving outside of the confinement of any previous "boxes."

During her work, she gets to transmit highly transformative energies that serve as a powerful catalyst for change. Her clients find themselves easily moving beyond life-long limiting patterns, and report feeling activated, calm, spacious, light, and happy.

As a global visionary, she often offers a fresh perspective to controversial topics, and is well versed in holding big energies, expanding into new possibilities, and surfing the edge of consciousness. She is not only hopeful but also excited about the new world she sees emerging.

Claudia's active journey into the world of coaching and consciousness began in 2007, when she completed her studies as a Happiness Coach at the Ella Kensington Institute in Germany. Her intuitive capacities began fully activating shortly after she graduated from the Enwaken Intuitive Leadership Program in Colorado a couple of years later. In addition, she has immersed herself in a wide variety of spiritual teachings and transformational modalities.

She is a native of Germany; an international workshop leader; the host and creator of the "Luminous Leader Academy" Tele-Summit; a soon-to-be podcast host; and an original founding partner of C-Synergy Career Coaching.

She has been guided to live on the beautiful Big Island of Hawaii, and invites you to join her on these powerful lands of raw creative power and sweet mamma love for your own personal life-changing retreat.

*Love*Bytes is her first book.

If you are interested in working with her personally, booking her as a speaker or guest on your podcast, or learning more about her Hawaiian retreats, you can email her at hello@ claudiasasse.com

Her virtual home is at www.ClaudiaSasse.com

# *IN GRATITUDE*

The transformational and creative power of opening our heart, love, and deep gratitude is a golden thread that keeps weaving through the story. Why don't you breathe into this with me for just a moment? What if, right now, you open up to receiving the energy of what you are grateful for in your life — past, present, and future — as I share my gratitude with you?

Thank you, spirit team, for your magical invitation to co-create and for gifting me this story to write. Thank you, Melissa, sister of my heart and energy-collaborator extraordinaire, for helping me reactivate one of my childhood dreams to become an author and write stories. You ignited the spark, cheered me on, kept seeing my highest potential, immersed yourself in a first edit, and a part of you even showed up as Laura throughout the story. I am eternally grateful for our friendship, your love, and your unwavering support.

Thank you, Sona, for your enduring friendship, your magic, your elixirs, and for connecting me to the stars in a whole new galactic and enlightening way. Thank you, fellow writer Sara L. Daigle (Alawahea and Triangle), for tracking along with the unfoldment of the story and giving me your amazing in-depth feedback. Thank you, Christine (www.ChristineLaria.com), playmate in the magical energies of Hawaii, crystalline sound magician, and embodiment of New Earth possibilities, for taking my headshot photo on one of the Big Island's most magical beaches and assisting me in staying spacious and connected.

Thank you, Ray, for waking me up in many ways, and providing the safe space to experience what it truly feels like to soften into opening my heart. Thank you, George, for your love, our deep, beautiful heart connection, guiding me to many amazing places, inspiring poetry, and being the embodiment of J in so many ways. Thank you, Hector, brother of my heart and soul, for your strength, sincere love of humanity, unshakable connection to spirit, and gifting me one of your stories to write. Thank you, Curt, for your many delightful gifts, for your encouragement, for always moving ahead in that space of expanded yet realistic possibilities, and for introducing me to the physical representation of what my true home looks and feels like — the juicy, rich, and expanded version of it. Thank you, Ken, for having your magnificent spirit come through as the Wise Man and giving me permission to use your name.

Thank you, Michel, for sailing through this adventure called life with me, for being my rock, for loving me unconditionally, for always looking out for me — often knowing what I need before I do — for taking care of the details, for your patience, your clear knowing, your wisdom and your loving reflection, for your generosity and sponsoring *LoveBytes'* publishing journey, and for your incredibly deep, big, loving heart.

Thank you, Ty — the way you move through life with clear direction, kindness, and dedication, while still knowing how to have fun and thoroughly enjoy yourself, is inspiring. Thank you, Noah, for your wisdom, deep love, kind heart, fun, and a little quirky way of being; for opening more of the world of your generation to me, and for continuously challenging me to see life with different eyes. So proud of both of you, and so happy you chose me to be your mom.

Thank you, Mom, for your love, your enthusiasm, your constant support, and your courage to expand and evolve at such an incredible pace over the last few years that you can actually track along and receive the message and the energy of this slightly unusual book.

Thank you, Dirk and Susan, for some great conversations and input, and for your assistance in creating those first translation attempts into German.

Thank you, James, for helping me convert "Love All" to binary code. And finally, thank you, book developer and creative midwife Naomi Rose (www.NaomiRose.net), for your kind, capable, and beautifully loving final editing touch so that *Love*Bytes could be birthed.

And a very special thanks to YOU! Thank you for joining me on this journey home, for immersing yourself in the transformational energies of the story. LoveBytes is a living transmission, which means it is alive in the way that its energies will continue to expand and evolve, as the collective consciousness of those who read it expands and evolves. So you are part of this evolution. Thank you for this, and thank you for all of your beautiful contributions as we create a new, life-affirming way of living on our planet — together.

www.ClaudiaSasse.com

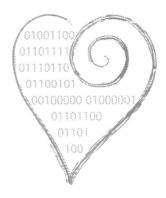

Printed in the United States
by Baker & Taylor Publisher Services